"Mason was right about you," she said. "I should've made an effort to know you sooner."

Derek opened his arms, pulling her easily into a hug. "I'm glad to know you now. And I don't want you to worry. You and Bonnie are going to be okay. That's a promise."

She leaned carefully against his chest, snuggling Bonnie between them and willing the words to be true.

"Mason started telling me about you the moment you came to stay with your grandma," Derek said. "He thought you walked on water."

Allison laughed. "Right now it feels like I'm barely keeping my head above the current."

"How about this, then?" he asked, voice low and tender. "I'll be your life raft for a little while, and you can be my anchor."

Her heart melted, and for the first time since they'd met, she knew precisely how much it would hurt when she had to let him go.

KENTUCKY CRIME RING

JULIE ANNE LINDSEY

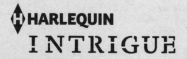

HARLEQUIN

INTRIGUE

For Laura Steurer

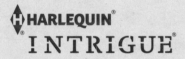

Recycling programs
for this product may
not exist in your area.

ISBN-13: 978-1-335-48916-6

Kentucky Crime Ring

Copyright © 2021 by Julie Anne Lindsey

This edition published by arrangement with Harlequin Books S.A.

For questions and comments about the quality of this book,
please contact us at CustomerService@Harlequin.com.

Harlequin Enterprises ULC
22 Adelaide St. West, 40th Floor
Toronto, Ontario M5H 4E3, Canada
www.Harlequin.com

Printed in U.S.A.

Julie Anne Lindsey is an obsessive reader who was once torn between the love of her two favorite genres: toe-curling romance and chew-your-nails suspense. Now she gets to write both for Harlequin Intrigue. When she's not creating new worlds, Julie can be found carpooling her three kids around northeastern Ohio and plotting with her shamelessly enabling friends. Winner of the Daphne du Maurier Award for Excellence in Mystery/Suspense, Julie is a member of International Thriller Writers, Romance Writers of America and Sisters in Crime. Learn more about Julie and her books at julieannelindsey.com.

Books by Julie Anne Lindsey

Harlequin Intrigue

Heartland Heroes

SVU Surveillance
Protecting His Witness
Kentucky Crime Ring

Fortress Defense

Deadly Cover-Up
Missing in the Mountains
Marine Protector
Dangerous Knowledge

Garrett Valor

Shadow Point Deputy
Marked by the Marshal

Impact Zone

Visit the Author Profile page at Harlequin.com.

CAST OF CHARACTERS

Allison Hill—New mother and friend of a recent murder victim, determined to help name and capture his killer before she or her baby become the next victim.

Derek Winchester—Oldest of the Winchester siblings. This PI is falling fast for the woman and baby who crashed into his life. Now he's protecting them with his.

Bonnie Hill—Allison's infant daughter.

Blaze Winchester—West Liberty homicide detective, assigned to Mason Montgomery's murder case.

Lucas Winchester—West Liberty special victims detective, assisting his brothers in the capture of Mason's killer.

Cruz Winchester—Derek's partner at their PI firm, a cousin by blood and brother by upbringing. He's always willing to help his family any way he can.

Mason Montgomery—Friend of the Winchester and Hill families, murdered while trying to help an injured woman on the run.

Redmon Firth—A criminal involved in the disappearance of multiple women and suspect in Mason Montgomery's murder.

Chapter One

Allison Hill tucked her infant daughter, Bonnie, into the cloth baby sling around her torso and moved swiftly through the cool morning wind. April in Kentucky was beautiful but brisk, and Allison had a little work to do before she went inside. Normally, her elderly neighbor, Mason, met her on the porch when he heard her truck rock down his long gravel drive, but today he'd stayed inside. He hadn't answered the door when she knocked, but the phone line was busy, a sure sign he was tied up on a call.

Mason was one of the few people Allison knew who still had a landline, attached to the wall by a spiral cord, no less. And he refused to get call-waiting because he claimed he could only talk to one person at a time. That person was usually his daughter, Franny, who lived in Minneapolis and worried desperately about her father living alone after his recent heart attack.

Allison hurried along the side of the home and into the shady backyard, ready to feed Mason's chickens and collect the eggs from his henhouse.

She'd promised Franny she'd handle the tasks during Mason's recovery. Another family friend was handling Mason's lawn mowing and prepping the ground for his garden.

The sound of the river mixed with the blustering wind as Allison approached the henhouse. The ground was soft and muddy from a late-night storm. She curved a protective arm over Bonnie as the insistent wind picked up, then pulled her baby's knit cap more securely over her soft blond curls. With only a few days left in her twelve-week maternity leave, Allison was already mourning the loss of her extended alone time with Bonnie. Thankfully her job at the day care would keep them close, even after she returned to work.

Allison let herself into the gated area around the henhouse, then headed for the little ramp. The chickens swarmed her legs, clearly recognizing her as their morning food source. She took off the lid of the tote of seed and scattered a few scoops over the ground. The hens lost immediate interest in Allison, clucking and diving over one another instead, eager for first dibs on breakfast.

She squatted to pluck a square of paper off the ground that had been trampled into the dirt by twenty chicken feet. "Litterbugs are the worst," she told Bonnie. She tucked the scrap into the pocket of her old zip-up hoodie, then put away the container of food.

A set of muddy footprints caught her attention as she hooked a basket for egg collection over the crook of her arm. The prints were strangely small, closer to her size than Mason's, and she could see the small outlines of toes. Her brow wrinkled at the thought. Bare feet? In an old man's henhouse? It wasn't warm enough to be without shoes right now, and the ground had been hard until the storm.

Strange.

Allison finished collecting eggs, then headed for the back porch, eager to know if Mason realized he'd had company.

She'd barely left the henhouse before getting her answer. More prints came quickly into view near the porch. These prints were accompanied by a trail of larger, heavier marks, likely made by a pair of men's boots, and about a million of the usual doggy tracks, courtesy of Mason's geriatric hound, Clark. Allison followed the path to Mason's door, then knocked. Maybe the man who cared for Mason's lawn had brought a barefoot child or wife along yesterday?

Allison knocked and the door swung open beneath her touch. A shiver of unease crept down her spine. "Mason?" she called, slipping into the kitchen. Her toe nicked a small white button, and Allison bent to pick it up. The button was delicate and flower-shaped. Nothing like the buttons on any of Mason's flannel shirts. Maybe the button belonged to whoever had made the footprints.

Her breath caught as she eased upright and took in the normally tidy space. Mason's countertops were littered with bloody rags, bandages and cloths. A first-aid kit had been ripped open, its contents splayed across the nearby table. A bottle of peroxide was lying in the sink. "Mason?"

Allison rushed into the living room, where the wall-mounted phone's receiver hung by its spiral cord. Abandoned. "Mason!" Her voice was loud and frantic, stirring Bonnie from her sleep.

A sense of doom spread in her stomach as she rushed through the old farmhouse, throwing open the doors and calling. Then, in a small room at the end of the hall, Mason's feet came into view. He was lying on the floor, eyes open and unseeing, his flannel shirt darkened with blood. "No!"

Allison dialed 911 on her cell phone as she fell to her knees at his side, patted his cold cheeks, then checked his neck for a pulse that wasn't there. Sobs broke across her lips as she cried the details into the receiver. "He's dead. I don't know. There's so much blood," she explained to the dispatch officer.

"I can't tell where he's hurt." She wiped wildly at her eyes, taking small sips of air and struggling to remain composed. Then, another thought came to mind. "Someone else was here. There are footprints in the yard, and I found a button on the floor."

"Are you certain you're alone now?" the dispatcher asked.

Ice ran through Allison's veins. "No." She'd raced around the first floor, but there was still an upstairs and basement. Both places she hadn't been.

And where was Clark? Not here, she decided, or he would be with Mason.

In the stillness, a couple of voices registered. "I hear people outside."

"Neighbors?" the dispatcher asked.

"There aren't any neighbors," Allison whispered. "Not like you mean. Not here." Allison's home was the closest to Mason's, and she was more than a mile away.

Allison crept to the nearest window and spotted a pair of men heading toward the home on foot. Two ATVs were parked in the trees beyond an aged outbuilding. The men scowled and barked at one another— short, snappy words, muffled by distance and the glass. Dark streaks smeared their shirts and arms.

"I see them through the window," Allison said. "I don't know them. And they might have blood on their clothes. What do I do?"

"Can you safely leave the premises?" the dispatcher asked. "I have the address, and units en route, but they're several minutes out."

Allison's gaze fell to Bonnie, fussy and squirming from the fear and tension surely rolling off her mother. "I think so," she said, determination rising in her core.

She was too late to help Mason, but she would protect her baby. Whatever the cost. Allison gave Mason a final look, her heart pounding in her throat. "I'm sorry," she whispered, then turned toward the hallway that had brought her to him. She reached the end of the narrow corridor and listened for any sounds indicating the men had entered the home. When silence prevailed, Allison sped back through the kitchen. "I parked in the driveway out front," she told the dispatcher. "I think the men went around back. I'm using the front door now." She clamped the phone between her ear and shoulder, then freed the dead bolt and swung the door wide.

Her truck glistened in the morning sunlight, waiting alone in the drive. Only a few yards away.

"Hey!" an angry voice called from behind her.

Allison froze, her hand on the open door, one foot already on the porch outside.

"Hold it right there." A heavy footfall sounded on the kitchen floor, two rooms away.

And Allison ran.

She tossed her phone into the sling with her baby, then bolted across the porch and down the short flight of steps, landing hard on the lawn. Allison wrapped a protective arm around the sling as she tipped forward, slamming her free hand and one knee into the earth.

Bonnie screamed.

"Stop!" the man demanded.

Allison surged forward, throwing herself ahead at full speed. She flung open the truck door and jumped inside, jamming her key into the ignition as Bonnie wailed. She pulled her daughter from the sling and moved her to the rear-facing car seat on the bench beside her. Her bumbling hands and flailing newborn made the job of fastening her safety belt almost impossibly difficult.

A gunshot exploded into the air. The thunderous sound echoed off the trees and hills.

"Get out of that truck," her assailant ordered, stalking predatorily across the porch. He lifted the gun in one outstretched arm, pointing it first at Allison, then swinging the barrel in the direction of Bonnie's car seat.

Allison jerked the vehicle into gear and jammed her foot against the accelerator, as the man's feet hit the lawn. Her old pickup launched forward, toward the gunman. A risky move, maybe, but far safer, in her opinion, than obeying the blood-smeared stranger.

He jumped back, screaming a string of curses as she pulled the shifter into Reverse and cranked the steering wheel. The truck spun in a wild backward doughnut through Mason's yard before rocketing forward down the driveway and onto the desolate country road out front.

The man took aim from a shrinking position in her rearview as Allison barreled away.

Her ears rang and her heart pounded.

Bonnie screeched beside her.

"It's okay," she breathed. "We're okay." Allison pried one hand away from the wheel to stroke her baby's tear-soaked cheeks. "You're all right. We're all right. Help is coming." Allison had gotten a good look at the man with the gun. She'd be able to describe him to the police when they arrived.

A flash of red caught her eye in the rearview mirror.

"Oh, no."

An ATV was racing along the road behind them.

Allison pressed the gas pedal with more purpose, then locked her doors. She needed to put as much distance as possible between her truck and the man giving chase.

The driver, visible in her side mirror, steered recklessly, a gun in one hand.

She slunk in her seat, fumbling to free her phone from the loose sling still hanging around her middle. "Hello?" she asked, praying the call hadn't disconnected.

"I'm here. Are you okay?" the dispatcher returned.

"No!" she screamed. "I am not okay! The intruder shot at me, and he's on an ATV now, chasing me!"

"Where are you?"

"In my truck. We're on River Road headed toward town." Allison raised her eyes to the rearview mirror, checking the ATV's progress. Four-wheelers were fast, but her little Ford was faster. She could get Bonnie and herself to safety. Everything would be okay.

A gunshot boomed, and Allison's truck jerked hard beneath her grip. The phone toppled from her hand as she clutched the wheel, attempting to regain control as her vehicle veered toward the hill on her right.

"He shot my tire!" Allison screamed, glancing at the floorboards and hoping the dispatcher could hear her. "I'm going to—"

The blast of a horn brought her eyes back to the road. Her little pickup had crossed the yellow line while she wasn't looking, and an enormous black truck with a large horse trailer was barreling right at her.

Allison jerked the wheel once more, and her truck hit a small roadside embankment, sending her briefly into the air before she crashed to a stop.

Chapter Two

Derek Winchester jammed his foot against the brake, likely laying thick streaks of tread on the asphalt. Some lunatic had crossed the yellow line right in front of him, then crashed into a ditch. The nut could've killed them both. Whoever it was had definitely ruined their ride. The pint-size pickup truck wouldn't come out of the wreck without some serious damage, and any amount of repair would cost more than the little red rust bucket was worth.

He slammed his shifter into Park, then flung open his door and jumped out, cell phone in hand.

The low hum of a distant ATV caught his ear, along with a small red dot vanishing in the distance.

"This is Derek Winchester. There's been a wreck on River Road," he told Dispatch when the call connected. "Single-car accident. An old Ford Ranger. I'm checking on the driver now. Probably texting. Send an ambulance and a tow truck."

Sirens split the air as Derek slid over the small hill on wet grass. "I hear them now. Damn. You're good, Casey," he joked.

"Funny," the dispatcher said. "Units were already headed your way. I'll send another set for the Ford Ranger. How many passengers?"

"Not sure. And we might've had another witness. There was an ATV," he said, stopping short at the sound of an infant's cry. "There's a baby on board," he said, adrenaline rushing through his system. He picked up speed as he moved over the small embankment. "Get those units out here."

He skidded to a stop, colliding with the driver-side door, then yanked the handle. Locked. A blond woman blinked dazedly at him, bleary-eyed and clearly shaken. Her truck was older than the invention of airbags, and her head had paid the price.

"Open up," he said. "You're hurt."

The baby's screams seemed to register before his words, and she jerked around to gather the infant from its seat.

"Stay back!" she warned, cuddling the infant to her chest and twisting to glare through the window. "Get away. The police are coming." A thick trail of blood slid over her forehead from a rising knot as she bent forward, stretching a hand to the floorboards. She came up with a cell phone. "Hello?" She frowned. "Darn it!"

Derek wrinkled his nose. "You were on your cell phone?" With a baby in the truck? And speeding? Was she kidding him? Fire ripped through his veins at the thought. Half his giant family was in law enforcement, and he'd seen firsthand the destruction that distracted drivers caused. He shook his head at the young mother, then refocused on the phone in his free hand. "She's conscious, but bleeding, and the baby's still crying," he told Casey. "No airbag. She took a solid hit to the head, but her truck's trashed, so she won't be driving again for a while."

The blonde tapped her window, drawing his attention. She waved a Taser from her side of the glass. "Get. Back," she demanded.

"She just threatened me," he said. "She might be on drugs. She looks a little crazed. She has a seat belt on, and the kid was in a car seat, so that's something. One of those bulky backward-facing deals. The ones with the dragster seat belts."

"Any visible injuries to the baby?" Casey asked.

Derek leaned closer, trying to get a look at the infant.

The woman shook her Taser again with one hand, while trying to comfort the baby pressed to her chest and also dial a cell phone with her opposite thumb.

"The crying has slowed," he reported, "but I'm not sure how safe it is in there with her, and she won't open the door." He gave the handle another pull for good measure, and the woman narrowed her crystal-blue eyes.

"Keep pushing me," she said.

Casey laughed. "I heard that. What happened, Winchester, you lose your charm in this fender bender?"

"Hey!" Derek called, ignoring Casey and knocking on the woman's window. "Is that even your baby?" he asked.

She scowled. A thread of confusion seemed to twist in her uncertain eyes.

"You running from the law or something?" he asked.

She tried to start the truck, but the engine was dead. She shot Derek a cautious look, then set aside the Taser and focused on her cell phone.

Another idea registered and Derek ground his teeth. Maybe this angelic, albeit bloody, blonde was the victim in some situation. "Did someone hurt you?"

She blinked, and her hands began to shake. Her tough expression crumbled. "I need an ambulance," she said. "For Bonnie." She hit Send on a call to 911 while Derek watched.

"I've already called them," he said, waving his phone at her.

She stilled, staring at his exposed screen. After a moment, she relented. "We're not getting out until an ambulance or a cop arrives."

"Fine."

She kissed the baby's head, unintentionally dislodging its knit cap.

Blood and tears dripped from the woman's face onto the infant's perfect blond curls. Her eyes widened as she tried to wipe them away, but they smeared. One trembling hand rose to her face, as if she only now realized she was bleeding. She stared at the blood on her fingers in disbelief.

"Casey?" Derek asked, suddenly less annoyed

with a potentially distracted driver, and curious about what he'd gotten himself into. "What's going on?"

The dispatcher sighed. "Help's on the way. Three minutes out."

"Don't even try that," he said. "I know all about your privacy laws and protocols. I don't want to hear that right now. I want to know what's going on. You said there were already units headed this way when I called. Why? Domestic violence? Infant abduction? Something worse?"

A parade of emergency vehicles came into view, then blew past him without slowing down. His horse trailer rocked on the roadside.

"That was Blaze's cruiser," he said, running the back of one hand over his eyes, then his mouth. "My brother's going somewhere hot. At least double the speed limit. I want to know why."

"He's dead." The words warbled though the glass, a soft gasp from the injured woman. "Someone killed him. I found him. They chased us. Shot at us." She pressed a hand to her face, quieting herself as the baby worked its tiny face into a knot.

Derek turned at the waist, watching the emergency vehicles vanish into the distance. There were only a few homes on this stretch of road, and one of them belonged to someone he'd known all his life. "Who?" The word fell from his tongue like a stone.

Her lips quivered, and her pale blue eyes filled with tears. "Mason Montgomery."

The shock of the words nearly knocked Derek off his feet.

The flashing lights of a cruiser and ambulance arrived before he could gather his wits, or his next full breath. Derek disconnected with Casey, then marched woodenly up the slick embankment to meet the responders and repeat what he'd just been told.

Officer Flint wasn't surprised. "I heard the call," he said soberly, clapping Derek on his shoulder as he passed. "I'm real sorry, man. I know your families are close. Blaze is headed to Mason's place now."

Several minutes later, Derek had learned the names of the woman and her baby—Allison and Bonnie Hill—and the details of their morning. Allison had answered Flint's questions as the paramedic, Derek's cousin Isaac, examined her and her daughter. Thankfully, both ladies would be okay, but Derek couldn't make sense of the news about Mason. He'd just seen him yesterday, and everything had been fine.

Allison had also explained that the ATV he'd seen racing away was more than a witness. The driver had shot out Allison's tire, causing her to lose control. If she'd gone off the road on her side, she and her sweet baby would be dead, like Mason, instead of shaken with minor injuries.

The tow truck arrived next, and Allison cringed at the sight of her pickup being dragged back onto the road. Derek didn't blame her. The front-end damage wasn't pretty.

Officer Flint made his way back to the ambulance with a bulbous infant car seat in his hand. "You're going to want to replace this as soon as possible. It'll get you home, but these seats aren't recommended for reuse after an impact like it just took." He shifted his gaze to Bonnie, sleeping in her mother's arms. "I'm glad for the work it did, but better safe than sorry."

"I have a second seat," Allison said. "I'll get rid of that one as soon as I'm home."

Flint nodded. "You need a ride?"

"I can take her," Derek said, speaking up before she could answer. "She needs to talk to Blaze at Mason's place, and I'm headed there now."

Flint shifted his weight. "That all right with you?" he asked Allison. "You can always go down to the station tomorrow to speak with Detective Winchester, or he can visit you when he's finished at the crime scene."

Allison pressed her lips together. She looked at her daughter, then Flint, then Derek.

Isaac offered her a reassuring smile. "Derek's okay," he said. "You should only go back to Mason's if you feel up to it, but for what it's worth, he's a good guy. A little grouchy sometimes, but he's family, so we put up with him."

Flint grinned. "You, on the other hand," he told Allison, "don't have to. I'm happy to take you wherever you'd like."

Allison fixed her narrowed gaze on Derek. "You're family?" she asked. "I don't see a resemblance."

Derek crossed his arms. "That's because Isaac got the good looks. I got the brains and brawn."

Isaac snorted, turning to pack up his things.

"We're cousins, technically, but we were raised together. Big, tight, crazy family. The detective up at Mason's is Blaze, Derek's brother. You're in good hands."

Derek watched as Allison considered the information. Her long blond hair was blowing in the wind around her face. Her cheeks were pink, and her bottom lip was red from biting. He tried not to imagine biting it for her.

Not an easy task.

At first glance, she seemed small and helpless, but he doubted that was true. The way she looked at her baby, with an odd mix of tenderness and ferocity, spoke volumes. In fact, he was darn thankful her truck door had been locked when he'd first reached her. Otherwise, he might've been Tasered for trying to rescue them.

"What?" she snapped. "Why are you looking at me like that? What are you thinking?"

Isaac's smile grew, and Flint chuckled.

Derek shrugged, unnerved by her apparent hostility toward him, and their audience. "I was thinking you're very pretty when you're not threatening to Taser me."

Her jaw dropped.

Derek gave himself a little internal kick for letting her get to him. She didn't have to trust him or ride with him. She didn't have to like him or talk to him ever again, for all he cared, but he needed to get moving. He pulled his emotions into check and dug the truck keys from his pocket. It was time to see what Blaze was learning at Mason's place.

Isaac closed the ambulance's bay doors, then stroked Bonnie's head. "Aspirin for pain. Hot and cold packs on your neck and shoulders as needed. Rest. Fluids. Follow up with your doctor and pediatrician. And don't worry about Derek. You aren't the first woman who's wanted to Taser him."

Allison smiled, and her expression was magic.

Derek pulled his gaze away from her mouth. "I'm going to Mason's. You're welcomed to ride with me, or take Flint up on his offer. Either way, I want to get moving." He spun the key ring on one finger, then angled away from her and shook the officer's hand in goodbye.

"Wait…" Allison's sweet voice drew a smile over his lips.

He turned back slowly, carefully wiping the pleasure from his face before she saw.

She marched stoically forward, poorly hiding a small limp. "There's no sense in asking Officer Flint to take me somewhere you're already going." She lifted her chin in defiance.

Trying to look tough, he realized.

Derek extended an arm in Flint's direction.

The officer passed him the car seat, then Derek carried it to his truck. A pretty lady and a baby in his wake.

Chapter Three

Allison did her best to look braver than she felt. She was sore and terrified. Her head pounded. Her neck ached, and her knee had hit the console during her crash hard enough to give her trouble when she walked. Immediate physical pains aside, her mind was a runaway train. What if the paramedic was wrong and Bonnie was seriously hurt? What if she had shaken-baby syndrome from the impact? What if Derek had an accident taking them home, and her car seat failed to protect her this time? Even tucked into his mammoth beast of a truck, injuries were possible. Bonnie was only eleven and a half weeks old. She could get hurt just falling off a couch.

Allison watched the passing scenery with growing dread. The familiar world outside, which had always seemed so beautiful before, was suddenly tainted. The winding road, lined with stubborn Kentucky wildflowers, would be forever tied to memories of fleeing the scene of Mason's murder. Being chased and shot at by a killer.

Emergency vehicles came into view around the

next bend. They were parked along Mason's property and in his long gravel drive.

Her chauffeur eased his ridiculous truck and giant horse trailer onto the berm and settled the engine. He'd given her a dozen sideways looks as he'd driven, as if she was an alien, or was still thinking of Tasering him, but he hadn't spoken.

Probably for the best.

Derek Winchester was unfairly handsome with the tanned, muscled body of a rodeo-magazine cover model. His fitted jeans were nearly as distracting as his square jaw and tough-guy disposition. He smelled of earth and hay, and there was enough mud on his boots to prove they weren't a fashion statement.

He was the groundwork for her wildest dreams, and she didn't have the luxury of dreaming, or sleeping, right now. Right now, her life was consumed by new motherhood.

"You okay?" Derek asked, leaning in her direction. The brim of his hat cast an air of mystery over soulful brown eyes.

"Yep." She unlocked her door and got out.

Alcoholics should avoid going to bars. Allison should avoid riding in pickup trucks with handsome cowboys. Her personal drug of choice.

A serious-looking man in a black ball cap and West Liberty PD windbreaker approached immediately. "Ms. Hill?" he called over the blowing wind. His gaze jumped from her to Derek as he rounded the truck's hood to her side.

Allison extended her hand.

"I'm Detective Winchester, West Liberty Homicide," he explained. "How are you doing? I hear you were in an accident." He skimmed her face and figure with quick, trained eyes. "And your little girl?"

"We're okay," she said, turning for the back door to Derek's truck cab. "Or, we will be."

Derek stepped into her path. "I've got this."

She waited, lips pressed, while he removed Bonnie, who was in her carrier, and held the seat in Allison's direction.

"I'll carry her without the seat," she said, then unfastened Bonnie and tucked her baby into the sling she'd repositioned over her shoulder and across her torso. "Thank you," she added, a moment too late.

Derek shrugged, having already returned the seat to his truck and closed the door. "She nearly ran me off the road," he told the detective. "Trashed her truck."

"So I've heard." Detective Winchester hooked his hands over his hips, revealing a sidearm and holster beneath the jacket. "Sounds like you've been through a lot today. Are you sure you're up to this? I don't mind stopping by your place when I finish here, if you'd rather rest now. I'm sure Derek would be happy to take you home."

Derek made a noise in his throat.

Allison refused to look in the cowboy's direction, or acknowledge the sound, whatever it had meant. So far she'd met two of her savior's relatives, and she preferred both to him. "I can rest when we finish here. I want to go over everything while the details are fresh in my mind."

Detective Winchester offered a small smile and nod, then led the way inside.

She gave her statement as they walked, answering basic questions about the timeline and her reason for being at Mason's place. The brothers exchanged a look when she told them about her daily hen duties. "Franny asked me to help out," she told them. "Franny is his daughter." Her breath caught and she covered her mouth. "Has anyone called her? Does she know?"

"I'll call," the detective said. "After we finish here."

Allison's heart plummeted. Franny had been so worried about her dad when she left the last time. She'd begged Mason to come with her while he recovered, but he'd refused. She'd been worried about his health. Who could have ever imagined something like this? Not here. In their small rural community. Inside the West Liberty city limits, maybe. But not down River Road, where farmers ruled the roost and good old-fashioned values were the law of the land.

She caught a renegade teardrop with the pad of her finger as it fell from the corner of her eye. There was a time to lose her mind over the tragedies of the day, but it wasn't now. "Have you found Clark?" she asked, presuming the Winchesters would also be familiar with Mason's beloved hound dog.

The detective shook his head, only glancing briefly in her direction. "Not yet, but he's old, half-blind and hard of hearing. Could be he's out having a grand time, or fast asleep somewhere, clueless. He'll turn up by dinner."

Allison hoped that was true, prayed Clark's nose would lead him home, and the monsters who'd hurt Mason hadn't done the unthinkable to a loyal old dog. She followed the Winchesters through Mason's home, careful to avoid the crime-scene crew taking photographs and marking everything with little plastic, numbered teepees.

"Can you think of anything else?" Detective Winchester asked, pausing in the unused dining room. He removed a notepad from his jacket pocket and made some notations while he awaited her answer.

"No. I think I've told you everything. It all happened so fast. Some of it feels like a blur." She cuddled Bonnie, hating that her baby had to be involved in this in any way. And that Mason wouldn't be around to see her grow. Allison lifted her eyes to the detective, who was already watching her. "Can I ask you a question?"

He dipped his chin. "Anything."

"What happened to Mason?" She'd been trying to make sense of it, but things hadn't added up. "There was a lot of blood. On his shirt, the bandages and cloths in the kitchen, but I didn't see any injuries on him. The man who chased me had a gun, but Mason didn't appear to be shot. If he had been, why did he try to bandage himself? Why not call 911, like I did? The phone was off the hook when I came in, but a man well enough to treat his own wounds could surely dial a phone. It doesn't make sense."

"Because it's not his blood," the detective said. "We think he had a heart attack. Mason had significant defensive wounds and bruising on his chest. He was likely shoved and or punched several times before his heart quit."

Derek seemed to shrink beside her. "Who the hell would attack a seventy-year-old man recovering from a heart attack? Why? Mason didn't have anything he wouldn't give away if someone asked him for it." He gripped the back of his neck and glared into the next room, where an officer snapped photos of the cluttered kitchen countertop.

"Whose blood was it?" Allison asked, fitting the new information into what she already knew. "And where did that person go?"

Derek swung his attention to her, his dark eyes alight with interest. "You think he was trying to help someone," he said. "That sounds like him. Are you sure he was alone when you got here?"

"No." Allison shook her head. "I only checked the first floor. Once I found Mason, I stopped looking and called the police. But there were footprints," she said. "Out back. In the mud and on the porch."

"We saw those," the detective answered. He looked to his brother. "Based on size and depth, they were likely made by a woman. The boot prints beside those were Mason's."

Memories of the footprints flashed into Allison's mind. The sensation of opening Mason's door and calling for him, unsure what she would find, sent goose bumps down her arms. Then she recalled her shoe colliding with something on the floor. "I found a button," she said, shoving a hand into her pocket. "I picked it up in the kitchen, before I saw the blood, and went looking for Mason." She handed the flower-shaped button to the detective.

He turned it over in his palm.

"So where is this woman now?" Derek asked. "And who were the men who came for her?"

Detective Winchester dropped the button into a small plastic bag, then set it on the dining-room table. "We've got two sets of heavy boot prints coming and going from the trees to the home. A size eight and a size twelve."

"Eight is small for a man," Derek said. "Any bare footprints?"

"No."

"Could one of the men have carried her," he suggested.

The detective waved an arm toward the back door. "Why don't we take a look?"

Allison hurried after them, curiosity flaring, as they crossed the porch to the backyard. "How will Derek know, if you don't?" she asked.

"Because I'm a tracker." Derek answered the question clearly intended for his brother, and he didn't bother turning around as he spoke. "I'll know if one set is deeper on the return trip."

"Because he'd be a hundred or so pounds heavier from carrying the woman," she concluded. "Smart.

This is where I saw the ATVs parked when I looked through the window."

Derek squatted over the footprints, near two distinct sets of tire tracks among the trees.

His brother hung back and focused on Allison. "Mason was important to us," he said, "and I know Franny. I want to call when I can be there for her and not have to rush off the line. I don't want you to think I was being cold earlier. Putting the job ahead of the people."

"I didn't," Allison said. "I assumed it was protocol or something."

He gave a sad smile. "I know he meant a lot to your grandmother and you. He talked about you both quite a bit."

Allison felt her brow wrinkle. "Really?"

"He was waiting for your baby to be born like she was his own granddaughter. It's nice to put faces with the stories."

His words raised a lump in Allison's chest. Her eyes stung, and she struggled to squash the feelings. Bonnie squirmed in the sling, and Allison stroked her sweet cheeks. "That's nice to hear. Thank you," she said. "He's been bragging about someone named Jack. He's caring for the land while Mason recovers. Is that a member of your family? Because I'm pretty sure he's the son Mason always wanted." And the guy Mason had been trying to set her up with for two years.

The detective rubbed a hand over his mouth, eyes fixed on Derek. "I think you've already met Jack."

Allison watched Derek's expression as he pointedly ignored them. Grief and determination warred on his brow. Her stomach tightened.

"You're Jack?" She looked from brother to brother. "I don't understand."

"It's a nickname," Derek said. "Mason loved nicknames."

"Yeah," she agreed. "I know."

"He thought I was a jack-of-all-trades when I played three sports in high school. And I'm taller than my brothers, so he thought 'Jack and the Beanstalk' applied. Though, using his logic, I'd be the beanstalk."

"We were sorry to hear about your grandmother," the detective continued. "We didn't know her, but Mason took it hard. They'd been friends for fifty years."

Derek's eyes narrowed to slits. "You're 'Alice in Wonderland'?" The words were flat and a little cold, adding an unpleasant edge to the sweet nickname Mason had tagged her with as a child.

"That's me," she answered, returning Derek's stubborn glare. "Allison Wonderland," she clarified. "Mason thought that was a hilarious play on words, by the way." Not something to snarl about. "And he said I looked like the character."

Derek rose to a standing position, dusting his palms.

The detective laughed. "I guess a new round of introductions are in order. I'm Blaze the Inferno."

An unexpected laugh bubbled through her. "Nice to meet you."

"Mason thought Blaze was a weird thing to name a kid, so he tried to make light of it. I'm not a pyromaniac or anything," he joked.

"Good to know. Okay. Wow. I feel like I've known you guys for years." Her throat tightened once more. Mason's approval of the brothers made them feel like friends instead of total strangers. And she could use a friend or two today.

"Same here," Blaze said.

Allison released a steadying breath, then looked at Derek with fresh eyes. "You're the local private investigator, security guy and horse whisperer?" She hated to point it out, but that jack-of-all-trades thing went well beyond playing multiple sports in high school.

Derek tipped his hat, still frowning.

She rolled her eyes.

A uniformed officer on the back porch waved his hand overhead. "Detective?"

"Excuse me," Blaze said. "You can head home, Allison. I know you're beat, and I'll reach out soon." He took a few purposeful strides toward the house before slowing his pace and calling over his shoulder. "Derek. She's the closest thing we have to a witness. Keep an eye on her?"

Allison gaped as Blaze turned and jogged to the porch without another word.

Hairs rose on the back of her neck as the implication set in. "Why did he say that? Does he think the killer could have recognized me somehow?"

Derek moved to her side, thumbs hooked beneath his belt. "Maybe. Or the guy who chased you down River Road could track you by your truck's license plate number. He must've had a good look at it."

Her arms curved protectively around Bonnie in the sling. She held her closer and pressed a kiss to her baby's head. "Can they really do that?" she whispered, her voice wobbling over the words. "They aren't cops. Not everyone has access to that kind of information."

"Criminals can do all kinds of things," he said. "Most of them are no good."

She raised her eyes to his, hoping to find reassurance. "Should I be worried?"

"Depends," he said, returning her stare. "It's been my experience that murderers hate to leave a witness behind. Does that worry you?"

Her stomach dropped, along with her gaze.

The trusting blue eyes of her precious baby girl looked back.

And a vise tightened on Allison's heart. "I can't defend her against two men," she whispered. "I'd be no match for them in a fight, and I don't own a gun."

"Doesn't matter," he said, crossing his arms and moving around to face her. "I never lose a fight. I'm a crack shot, and I'm not letting you out of my sight."

Chapter Four

Derek parked his truck on the long gravel lane to Allison's home. The small white two-story farmhouse had black shutters, probably less square footage than his stables and about an acre of lawn, surrounded by trees.

Beds of fresh mulch circled the porch, bookending the steps with spring flowers and brightly colored whirligigs. Aluminum pie tins bobbed on fishing line around a small gated garden at the home's side, and a bulbous yellow baby swing hung from the limb of a sturdy oak.

"How are the pie tins working for you?" Derek asked, tipping his head toward the garden. Making small talk wasn't his strongest skill, but he supposed after rudely inserting himself into her life for the foreseeable future, he should at least try to put her at ease.

No easy task since he so clearly irritated her.

Allison groaned. "That's not a garden. It's a wild-life food bank."

Derek rubbed a hand over his curving lips as she

led the way up the walk. As he'd suspected, the pie tins weren't fooling any animal.

Allison unlocked the door, then stepped aside and shot Derek a look. "Maybe you should check for gun-wielding lunatics before I take Bonnie inside." She'd tucked her baby into the sling once more, and snuggled her against her chest.

"Sure." Derek nodded and stepped past her, into a small living room. He should've been the one to suggest checking the house before allowing her and her baby inside, but she'd beaten him to it. What was going on with him? He knew how protective details worked. "I can't decide if I'm honored you trust me to do the job or offended you've offered me up to take the first bullet," he said, hoping to cover his agitation.

"I'll let you decide," she said, motioning him to get started.

Derek smiled to himself as he took a spin through the tidy rooms. There were happy colors on the walls, in the accents and rugs. A direct contrast to his own home, done mostly in earth tones. The upstairs was smaller than the downstairs. Two bedrooms and a bathroom only. A nursery for Bonnie. And a room for her mom. Derek's gaze caught on a basket of freshly folded laundry at the end of a neatly made bed. Lacy scraps of colorful fabric caught his eye, and he rubbed a hand over his forehead, scrubbing away the immediate, but unbidden images.

A wall of framed photos made him slow his pace on the way back downstairs. Allison starred in most of the shots, often with a woman he vaguely recognized as her grandmother. Many more with Allison's baby. He couldn't help wondering where her parents were. And Bonnie's father, for that matter. Not that any of it was his business.

Allison was beautiful, in a girl-next-door way. A country-girl way. With long blond hair falling down her back, those big blue eyes and freckles. In the photos, she wore cut-off jean shorts with ball caps and boots. She perched on rocky peaks and sat on docks with a fishing pole. She made life look easy. Enjoyable. Made the world around her look good. Instead of infested with danger and the kind of deranged people who'd kill a sick old man inside his home.

A lump formed in Derek's throat at the sudden reminder, and he was instantly thankful for an extra moment alone as pain welled in his chest.

"Derek?" Allison called, signaling he'd been gone too long.

"Yeah," he said, jogging back down the steps. "You have a basement?"

Allison pointed to a door beyond the kitchen, and Derek opened it.

He flipped the light switch, then went down the steps. He was back in a flash. The basement was as clear and open as every other room in her home. Only a few stacks of labeled totes and boxes occupied the large square space. Nowhere to hide. "All good," he said, shutting the door once more.

Allison moved into the front room and closed the door. "Thanks for doing that."

"It's no trouble," he said. "Odds are, whoever was chasing you is halfway across the state by now."

"If he's not?" she asked.

Derek flashed a confident smile. "Then he'll soon wish he was. I'm here. You can breathe easier for now."

"And what about later?" she asked. "I live here, alone, with an infant. It's not like you can move in until the killers are caught. They might never be identified, let alone found."

Derek groaned internally. She was right, of course, but saying so wouldn't bring her any comfort. He moved his hat to his chest, then dragged a hand through his hair, at a loss for the words she needed.

"What?" she demanded. "I'm right to be upset."

"You are," he agreed. "I'm trying to think of something helpful to add, but this isn't my best event." Just ask his mother. Or any of the women he'd dated. "When I'm upset, I usually have some whiskey or go fishing. Maybe take one of the horses out for a ride. I'm doubting any of those suggestions will work here. Unless I can get you some whiskey?" he asked, hopefully scanning the cheery yellow kitchen.

Allison snorted, then blew past him to the refrigerator. "Be serious." She yanked open the freezer door. "This is a job for ice cream. Care to join me?"

His mouth quirked in response. "Absolutely."

Derek added resilience to a small list of things he'd noted about Allison since they'd met. It seemed like much more than a few hours since then. He'd assumed her reckless when she'd run off the road in front of him. But she was actually fierce. She'd outrun a gun-toting killer, with a baby in tow. And she'd returned to the scene of a friend's murder while the pain was still so fresh. Just so she could try to help. She'd kept up easily as he'd discussed the evidence with Blaze, and she'd made some good assumptions of her own. A very different picture than he'd originally painted of her.

"Want to sit outside to eat?" she asked as she handed him a bowl of ice cream, then dragged the back door open.

"Sure," he answered, his gaze trailing her onto the porch.

He couldn't help wondering what sort of picture she'd painted of him.

She set her bowl on a porch swing, then lowered Bonnie into a portable crib to rest.

Derek followed her lead, lifting her bowl out of the way so they could sit and swing.

Her hands shook as she accepted the dessert, then she poked it with her spoon.

"You okay?" he asked, knowing it was a ridiculous question—how could she be? But he hoped to sound attentive and kind in response to her hospitality.

She swept long straight hair away from her shoulder and nodded absently, her gaze drifting to the little crib. "I'm going to be."

"You want to talk about it?" he asked, dipping his spoon into the bowl and stretching out his legs. This was the part where his brothers would say no, then pour another shot of whiskey.

"I hate that Bonnie was with me today," Allison said. "She shouldn't have experienced any of that." The guilt and shame in her tone made him turn to face her.

Did she blame herself for some part of what happened?

"I keep thinking I should've gone over earlier this morning. Or maybe I should've checked on him last night. What if there was some way I could've helped him, and I missed my chance?" She wiped a tear off her cheek on a long exhale.

"Sometimes terrible things happened to great people," Derek said. He saw it all the time as a PI. And before that as a West Liberty rookie cop, and as a soldier.

"Do you believe in fate?" Allison asked, abruptly changing the subject, and the direction of his thoughts.

"What?"

"Destiny. Cosmic intervention. Universal signs that give us direction, as long as we're willing to look for them," she said, as if any of that made any sense.

As if Mason's murder was…what? His destiny?

Derek pushed another spoonful of ice cream into his mouth, reminding himself that she'd been through a trauma, and had to make sense of it however she could.

She stared, waiting. Her ice cream was melting, untouched in the bowl.

"Not really, no," he said after he ate another bite, when it seemed as if she wasn't moving on without his response.

"I do." Her tone was wistful, and her gaze flickered to her daughter. "I think there's a greater plan happening around us all the time. And that sometimes when we wonder why things happen to us, it's really not about us at all, but about the other person instead. Does that make sense?"

"No." He set aside his empty bowl, wanting to make an excuse to leave, check the perimeter of the land, or take a fake phone call to escape a conversation that was grating hard against his frustration and grief. "Are you talking about you now? Or Mason? Because I don't see how some greater good can come of his murder. Especially if he really was killed while trying to help someone," he snapped. A lump formed in his throat, stopping the words, and he forced his eyes away, willing himself to tighten up.

"I didn't mean to suggest that," she said quietly. "I only mean that I believe there's a purpose to everything, every encounter. Like, if he hadn't had a recent heart attack, I wouldn't have been helping him with his eggs, and it might've been a long while before someone checked on him."

"So?" Derek said, voice rough and sharp. "It was still too late." What did it matter if he was discovered now or three days from now?

"Too late to save him," she said, "but maybe it isn't too late to find the person who did this and save the girl," she said. "I saw the men's faces. Saw their

ATVs. You were able to examine their tracks. Once it rains, that evidence is gone. Timing matters," she said. "And if whoever Mason was protecting had run to someone else's home, the killers might never be caught. But she chose Mason. A quiet old man with a big heart and deep ties to a family of law enforcement. Maybe, because of him, that woman will be saved after all."

Derek carried his bowl into the kitchen, needing some space. His heart ached with grief and anger over the senseless loss of his friend's life. Finding the killer would be great, but it wouldn't change anything or even lessen the pain. Nothing would.

His phone buzzed in his pocket, and he pulled it free for a look at the screen.

"Hey," Derek answered, recognizing Blaze's number immediately. "How's it going over there?"

"As well as can be expected," Blaze said, a rumble of thunder rolling through the line and in the world outside Allison's door. "We were lucky to get here when we did. This rain is likely to wash away the tracks and evidence on the property."

Derek slid his eyes toward the open back door, his lips pulling low into a frown. Allison had just said something similar.

"We're wrapping up outside now," Blaze said. "We can take our time indoors, but I've got good and bad news. Clark came back. He seems fine. Filthy, but unharmed, and he knows something's wrong. But he hasn't stopped howling, and he's trying to get into the house, back to Mason. He's wreaking havoc over here, and I don't have a man to assign to doggy duty."

"Yeah," Derek said. "I'll come get him."

"Maybe take him over to your place," Blaze suggested. "Looks like he's been rolling in mud. Smells like he was rolling in something else."

Derek grimaced. "Great."

"You're going to want to hurry," Blaze said. "There's one hell of a storm brewing."

"I'll be there in ten." Derek disconnected, secretly thankful for a few minutes away. Emotions had no place in his line of work, and his were going haywire. He poked his head through the back door, catching Allison's attention.

"Everything okay?" She watched him, expectantly, still holding the bowl of melted ice cream.

"Yeah. Clark's back."

Her face lit with relief, and Derek's chest tightened in response, the unexpected emotion taking him by surprise.

"I've got to run back to Mason's and pick him up," he said. "Blaze says he's howling and looking for a way to get to Mason, causing trouble, and they're shorthanded. I can take him out to my place. Clean him up and get him some food."

Her fair eyebrows knitted. "No," she said. "Don't leave him alone again. Bring him here. He's probably confused and terrified. He knows Bonnie and me. Maybe that will be some comfort."

Derek looked around the charming, brightly colored home. "He's going to stink this place up and cover it in mud."

"I don't care." She fixed him with a no-nonsense look. "The immediate goal is to remove him from the crime scene, right? They're probably racing to beat the storm, too. Just bring him here, and we'll figure it out. It's the least we can do."

He looked from Allison to the sleeping baby. She was talking as if he planned to leave her alone after the morning she'd had. "You're coming with me," he said. "Maybe once you take a look at him in the condition Blaze described, you'll change your mind about dropping him off at my place."

Her brow furrowed, and she bit into her bottom lip, probably trying to picture two adults and an infant in the cab of his truck with a fat, filthy old hound.

She followed his gaze to Bonnie—she was clearly hating to disturb the baby after all she'd been through. "I'd like to see her sleep awhile longer."

The thunder rolled again, vibrating the world around them.

"We'll be back as soon as we can."

Allison dragged her attention back to Derek. "Can we stay?" she asked. "You said earlier that we were safe for now. How long does that last, exactly?"

He crossed his arms. He didn't like where this was going, and he couldn't exactly stuff her into his truck like luggage if she didn't want to go. But Blaze needed the dog away from the crime scene. He suppressed a swear.

It would take time for the shooter and his partner to regroup. Longer for them to access a database and gain information about Allison's license plates, assuming they were smart enough or had the connections to do it at all. Smart criminals would at least wait until after dark to strike again, especially with cops crawling all over Mason's home, a mile away. And smarter criminals would be across the state line by now, not sticking around to get caught.

"Fine," Derek said. "I'll grab the dog and be back with him in a few minutes. Lock the doors and windows. Stay inside and call 911 if you see, hear or sense anything is wrong. False alarms are better than the alternative every time."

She nodded and carried the portable crib inside, baby and all.

He collected her discarded bowl from the porch, then shut and locked the door while she settled the little crib in the living room.

"Hurry," she whispered, her bravado faltering as she walked him to the front door.

Derek fought the bizarre urge to kiss her goodbye. Maybe it was the strange connection they shared, after their recent and unexpected loss. Maybe it was something else he wasn't ready to think about. Regardless, touching her was inappropriate, and time was of the essence, so he tipped his hat, then headed for his truck at a jog. Already in a hurry to get back.

Chapter Five

Allison paced the rooms of her home, peering systematically through each window in search of external threats. She'd felt fine before Derek left, more concerned about her baby's rest than fearful of a second attack.

Until his truck vanished in the distance, and every manner of awful thing felt suddenly possible. Even imminent.

So she'd begun to make the circuit, checking the front and back lawns and side yards through the first-floor windows, then up the steps for a better view into the trees. The leafy canopy was thick and green this time of year, but with the breeze from the brewing storm, she was sure she'd be able to spot a pair of red ATVs.

She checked her watch as she returned to the kitchen, the way she did each time she completed the route. Barely a minute had passed since she'd last checked. Eighteen had passed since her protector had gone.

"Hurry," she whispered, sending the words out

like a prayer. Something about the darkening sky, the thunder and wind, the gooseflesh on her arms, told her there was trouble coming. Maybe it was her recent trauma and current fear talking, but she was sure she should take Bonnie and leave.

Except, she didn't have a truck. Hers was wherever the tow truck had hauled it away.

Images of the chase flashed in her mind, followed by a number of gruesome and terrifying images from her morning. Muddy footprints. Blood. Mason. Allison sucked in a ragged breath and tears began to fall. She'd held them at bay as long as possible, and now, alone in her home, with Bonnie asleep, she indulged herself with the release she so desperately needed. She cried softly into her hands as she slid to sit on the kitchen floor, back against the door.

She remembered the looks on the men's faces as they'd emerged from the woods. The hate in the shooter's eyes as he'd realized there was a witness. And that she was getting away. He hadn't hesitated to take a shot at her, even as she carried an infant.

She didn't want to think about what would've happened to Bonnie if Derek hadn't been on the road at the exact place and time when Allison wrecked. He'd been her unintentional savior, and she owed him dearly for that. Allison wiped her eyes and let her ragged breaths settle. Mason hadn't lived to see it happen, but her path had finally crossed with Derek's, and it had saved her life.

She pushed onto her feet, checking her watch once

more. Her shoulders sagged slightly in relief. Derek would surely be back any minute.

She didn't want him to leave again. At the very least, not tonight, but how could she ask him to stay?

Her stomach rumbled, and a perfect answer came to mind. She hadn't had more than a spoonful of ice cream since breakfast. And unless Derek had a bite while he off collecting Clark, then he hadn't had a decent meal, either. Providing a delicious dinner was something she could do for him. Butter him up, then beg him to sleep on her couch. It was a shameless plan that she was ready to put into motion.

She grabbed her grandma's recipe box off the top of the refrigerator and thumbed through it in search of the perfect meal. Grandma's chicken-fried steak was phenomenal. Everyone loved it, and Allison was good at making it. Served with mashed potatoes, there was nothing better, except maybe her mom's apple dumplings. It was hard to imagine a man built like Derek Winchester indulging in anything bathed in butter, battered or fried, but he'd accepted her ice cream, so dinner seemed worth a try.

The soft purr of an engine set her on alert, and she returned the recipe box to the fridge top. The sound wasn't a truck.

She listened closely, heart hammering as she tip-toed wildly through her home, searching for signs of an approaching ATV and praying she was wrong. The sound ended, and the thunder rolled. There were no signs of trespassers from any of her first-floor windows.

She took the steps two at a time, phone in hand, then peered through the upstairs windows, gaze locked on the blowing trees.

The ATVs she'd seen at Mason's were parked less than fifty yards out, and the riders were nowhere to be seen.

"No, no, no," she whispered, bursting from the room. She dialed emergency dispatch as she hit the top step and nearly fell down the rest in the process.

Three heartbeats later, her feet pounded across the kitchen floor. She grabbed her baby sling from the counter where she'd discarded it, then darted into the living room to collect Bonnie from the portable crib.

"West Liberty Dispatch," a woman answered. "What's your location and emergency?"

"Shh," Allison cooed, attempting to calm the infant she'd just jerked from a deep sleep, before her cries alerted the coming intruders. "This is Allison Hill," she said softly, slipping Bonnie into the swath of fabric against her chest. "I called earlier, after being chased by a shooter. I believe he's returned and is outside my house." She rattled off her home address as she sprinted toward the front door, prepared to make another desperate run for her...

"I don't have my truck," she whispered, panic threading through her chest and limbs. "I'm stuck in my house with my baby."

Bonnie was in danger, and they couldn't escape. The realization was an ax to Allison's heart.

"Do you have a visual on the man now?" the dispatcher asked.

"No." Allison scanned her home, her mind racing. "I don't want to look outside again in case I'm spotted. With my truck gone, it might look as if I'm not home." Except for the fact that the man who'd chased her saw her wreck. "I'm going to try to hide," she said. "How soon can someone get here? There are officers at Mason Montgomery's place. That's only a mile away."

"I have units en route. Stay on the line."

Allison slipped through her basement door, then shut it behind her and crept down her creaky steps, into the dark.

Bonnie fussed and whimpered, but had thankfully stopped crying.

"It's okay, sweetie," Allison whispered. "Mama's got you."

The sudden crack of splintering wood echoed above her, causing Bonnie to start. Her blue eyes were as wide as saucers in the musty basement. Her small cherub face was illuminated by light coming through two narrow glass block windows.

The intruders had probably kicked in her door, but Allison didn't dare speak to tell the dispatch operator.

Instead, she listened closely as heavy footfalls rocked overhead, and deep voices called for her to come out and play.

Allison rushed across the ancient concrete floor toward the row of lidded plastic containers, then ducked behind them. She patted the wall in search of the old root-cellar door, hidden behind the marked tubs of decorations and mementos. Her fingers found the rectangular wooden latch, then turned it gently, freeing the dilapidated old door.

The scents of damp earth and long-forgotten vegetables hit her with a resounding smack, and darkness overcame her as she tugged the root cellar's door shut behind her. When the home was built, more than a century ago, and until her grandmother was too old to comfortably maneuver the basement steps on a regular basis, the small dark room had been used to store extras from the garden harvest. Old wooden shelves lined one wall, filled with things that had been canned in warm weather to sustain her family through the cold. Now, the air was slightly dank and tinged with the afterthoughts of cabbage, onions and turnips.

Bonnie made a disgruntled noise.

"Shh." Allison nuzzled her closer, angling her baby's face toward her, hoping to provide more of her familiar mama-scent. Then, she peered through the small gaps between wooden slats in the door.

Without access to the light from her basement's narrow windows, the root cellar was like standing in an open grave, and the thought rattled her to her core. Surrounded in dirt and blackness, she pressed the silly fears of childhood from her mind. Mice and spiders. Worms and snakes. But nothing hiding with Allison in the dark possessed half the threat of the men overhead.

She closed her eyes, pressed a kiss to Bonnie's forehead and lifted the phone to her ear. "They're inside," she whispered.

"The men you saw earlier?" the dispatcher asked, instantly responsive.

Allison nodded, fumbling to lower the volume on her phone, the other woman's voice feeling like a scream in the silence. "Yes."

"How many? And how did they gain access?"

Above her, the deep voices grew agitated and hostile. Something shattered, and Bonnie whined.

"Shh." Allison peppered her baby's face with kisses, shushing and lightly bouncing her. "It's okay. I've got you. We're okay."

"Ms. Hill?" the dispatcher asked. "Can you tell me what's happening?"

The ceiling above her rattled as the men stopped abruptly, sending a shiver down her spine. Did they hear Bonnie? Could they hear the dispatcher? Had Allison whispered too loudly?

Another loud crash reverberated through the boards above them, shaking loose dirt onto Allison's hair and probably into Bonnie's face.

The baby squirmed and grunted. Then sneezed.

Allison winced.

Footfalls began again, the light thuds crisscrossing her home.

"No one's home," a voice said.

"Well, this is the place," the second voice said. "That's her in the pictures."

Allison's breaths came faster. Bonnie squirmed.

The familiar squeak of her basement door nearly stopped her heart.

"Ms. Hill?" the nearly forgotten dispatcher prodded. "Can you provide an update on your situation?"

Allison listened intently to the creaking basement steps, ears ringing as she ignored the tiny voice on her phone.

"Ms. Hill?"

"You hear that?" a man asked.

Allison pressed the phone to her chest, fear extinguishing the air from her lungs. She refocused on the slivers of space between slats on the cellar door. Beyond the pile of storage containers, a man passed through the shaft of light from her basement window. He had a gun in a holster at his side. A hunting knife in a sheath on his belt. And a folded length of rope in his hand.

"I think she's down here," he called boldly to his partner, still upstairs. "Hiding." He chuckled. "Are you hiding, baby girl? You ran from me once, but you won't get away this time. Not you or that sweet pink bundle of yours."

Above her, the ceiling bounced. Furniture scooted, and something broke.

The other man didn't respond. He was too busy. Destroying her home.

Her gut clenched, and her throat constricted as the man before her crept closer, scrutinizing the space.

"Come out, come out, wherever you are," he taunted. "You and I have unfinished business. First, I'm going to teach you a lesson or two. Then, you're going to wish you'd minded your own business." he snarled.

Bonnie squirmed and complained. A hearty grunt and burst of irritated babble broke free of her sweet lips, followed by a disgruntled half cry.

And Allison's heart stopped.

The man turned to face the row of bins, and a creepy, predatory smile spread over his partially shadowed face. "There you are," he said, striding eagerly in her direction.

Allison widened her stance and prepared to fight.

Chapter Six

The skies opened on Derek as he closed the truck door behind Clark. He'd had to lift the fat old hound onto the seat when he'd refused to climb in on his own. It wasn't that Clark didn't enjoy a good truck ride. More that his arthritis required a set of custom steps to climb into anything taller than a couch. He'd gotten the world's fastest bath, courtesy of Mason's outside water hose, before being rubbed down with some old work towels in Derek's truck. Now, the interior would only smell like a wet dog, not whatever carcass Clark had found to roll in.

Derek climbed behind the wheel with a mix of relief and urgency, in a hurry to get back to Allison and her baby. He gunned the engine to life. He'd promised Allison he'd be back within half an hour, and he was running behind. The truck growled hungrily as he tore back down the driveway. The horse trailer behind him slowed everything down. He'd been on his way to drop it off when he'd nearly run into Allison, and he couldn't wait to leave the heavy burden behind soon.

Hopefully, Allison had found a few minutes to rest and regroup while he'd been away. He hadn't pushed back when she'd asked to stay, because he wanted to give her the time and space she needed to collect herself after what was probably the most traumatic day of her life. And once he got back, he didn't plan to leave her side again anytime soon. Not unless she kicked him out, in which case, he'd keep watch from his truck like a stalker. But he wouldn't let his guard down once the psychopaths who'd killed Mason, and apparently abducted a woman, had time to figure out where Allison lived and come for her again.

If they came back. *If*, he reminded himself. He'd hung a lot of hope on the idea the criminals might be more interested in putting distance between them and local authorities than hunting down a single witness.

Rain pelted the windshield as he motored toward the little white farmhouse, intentionally ignoring the speed limit. Thankfully, the old county road was void of traffic to slow him down. He adjusted his wipers, then powered on the police scanner to listen for updates from Mason's place. Hopefully, Blaze hadn't finished up and headed over to Allison's yet. Derek didn't like the idea of them talking without him. *Not that Blaze would cross any boundaries*, he thought, wondering at his peculiar feelings on the subject. Obviously, it wasn't any of his business what either adult did or whom they spoke to. Plus, Blaze was in love, engaged and a new father. He was so obsessed with his fiancée, a team of naked cover models couldn't catch his attention, let alone capture his interest.

But why did Derek care if Allison caught his brother's interest?

An oldest brother's urge to keep the younger sibling in line? Loyalty to Blaze's fiancée?

Or something else?

He grimaced at the unfamiliar stirring in his core. Maybe he was the one who needed a moment to rest and regroup.

He should've asked Allison if there was anyone he could call for her. Someone she'd want to be with on a day as bad as this one, but he hadn't wanted to imply she needed the help. She'd struck him instantly as someone who took care of herself, and who'd likely take offense if anyone said otherwise. Still, he should've asked. The absence of her parents from photographs throughout her home made him wonder. Had she lost them, too? Didn't she have siblings? Cousins? Anyone other than her baby and grandmother, who was now gone? There was an army of Winchesters, spread widely and generously across the country. More than one hundred of them converged annually on an unsuspecting town of their choice, all in the name of a week-long reunion. And oftentimes, a week wasn't enough to get to spend any amount of real time with everyone.

Was it possible Allison was completely alone?

The idea tugged at him, but he tossed it aside. Everyone had someone. He was being silly and overly dramatic. Clearly, the day had taken a toll on him, too.

He petted Clark with his right hand as he drove. The old boy was miserable, and though the hadn't been allowed to see Mason, he clearly understood something was very wrong.

Behind him, Blaze's cruiser tore out of the drive, lights on and catching up fast.

Another cruiser followed.

Derek's hand jumped from Clark's wet head to the police scanner, cranking up the volume that had been barely more than a whisper.

"Repeat," the voice said. "We have a confirmed break-in at four-four-one-one River Road. Requesting assistance for a mother and infant child."

"Copy that," Blaze answered, giving his call sign and assuring he and Officer Flint were three minutes out.

Derek's heart pounded as he pressed his foot against the gas pedal with renewed purpose. His truck and its load rocketed forward, working hard to stay ahead of the cruisers in pursuit.

Allison's bruised face and small frame flashed in his mind. She was no match for one man. She wouldn't stand a chance against two.

Her long hair gave an attacker something to grab on to. A way to still and control her.

And her infant made her weak.

Derek had only known her a few hours, but he'd seen the look in her eyes as he'd approached her wrecked truck. She'd willingly comply with any request, however self-destructive, if the assailant promised not to harm the child. She'd walk away, into their possession, to her death.

He cussed and pounded the heel of one hand against the steering wheel, willing the truck to move faster on the rain-soaked road. Every protective instinct in him roared against the possibility of his imagined scenario.

He couldn't let them take her.

The truck ripped into her driveway. He slammed a palm against the horn as he unfastened his seat belt and jumped out, hoping to startle the intruders, make them scatter, leave her alone.

Clark tipped back his head and howled.

Derek shut the dog inside the truck for his safety.

Blaze and Flint arrived only seconds later, sirens raging.

Derek stormed onto the porch, gun drawn and thankful Blaze had arrived. He would take the time to think. Make a plan. Cover the other exits. Call for backup.

Derek turned the knob on the front door and swung it open, a single thought on his mind.

Save Allison and her baby.

Shards of splintered wood along the jamb confirmed he wasn't the first one to let himself in.

A moment later, Allison's scream split the air. Derek flew inside, muscles tight and senses on high alert. The tidy home had been trashed. Furniture overturned.

He froze and listened to the silence around him. *Come on, Allison. Scream one more time for me, baby.*

An infant's cry pulled Derek's attention to the open basement door.

Outside, a gunshot boomed.

Derek hurried to the basement, instinct clawing down his back, pushing him impossibly faster. The gun had been fired by Blaze or the officer, he told himself. His brother and Allison were safe. She was probably hiding with her baby.

"Allison!" he called, landing on the ancient concrete floor. The space was darker now than it had been earlier. Storm clouds had stolen the light from the narrow glass block windows.

Derek yanked an overhead chain, flooding the mess of scattered plastic totes and lids around him. The baby cried again, and Derek followed the sound.

She whimpered from the top of a stack of quilts, tucked safely inside an open container.

"Allison!" Derek turned in a slow circle, searching for the child's mother. No sign of Allison. No traces of blood, despite many indications of a struggle.

He swore, his heart aching.

She'd left the baby.

"Come on," he said, lifting the infant, still swaddled in the loop of material Allison had worn.

Her little red, tearstained face beat Derek's leathered heart into pulp. He raised the fabric, careful not to spill the baby, then looped it over his head and poked one arm through.

The baby stopped crying, her lip quivering, eyes wet with tears.

Suddenly, his gun seemed wildly inappropriate.

He holstered his sidearm, then gripped the baby, his softened heart racing in his chest. He rushed back up the stairs, then pulled out his phone to dial Dispatch. There had been a gunshot. If his brother had pulled the trigger, someone needed a hospital. The baby should definitely see a medic, if she didn't need a doctor. There weren't any visible injuries, but that meant little to someone so fragile.

Wind rattled the home as he crossed Allison's kitchen to the open back door.

Blaze was visible in the storm, moving slowly toward the trees. One hand rested on the butt of his gun. The other officer had his flank.

Derek dialed Dispatch and reported what he knew, then moved onto the porch, scanning the distance, where Blaze's attention was fixed.

Allison came into view, drenched and shaking beside an ATV thirty yards away. A man straddled the ATV, his broad forearm wrapped around her center. Blood trickled over the assailant's skin, staining Allison's shirt and reminding Derek of the single shot he'd heard earlier. The coward was using her like a human shield.

Derek gritted his teeth—he was desperate to act, to knock the son of a gun off that four-wheeler and show him what it felt like to be overpowered, outmatched and afraid.

Instead, he watched and waited in anger, rooted to the spot by a ten-pound baby at his chest.

"Don't come any closer," the assailant snarled. "I'll drag her to death by her pretty hair! I swear it!"

He revved the little vehicle's engine, as if to punctuate the threat.

Blaze and the officer stepped forward, feet moving in sync.

The officer kicked out one leg, dragging his boot through a shallow puddle forming in the grass. A gun appeared and bounced toward the porch. Possibly dropped during the assailant's attempted escape.

Allison's gaze latched onto Derek, and he focused on her features. She didn't look terrified, as he'd originally thought. She looked…angry. No. Determined. Her eyes moved down and to the right. Three fingers popped free of her fist. Then ticked down. One by one.

She'd initiated a countdown. To what?

Derek's attention jumped to Blaze and the officer. Did they see what she was doing?

She began to cry when all three fingers were curled once more, softly at first, then louder. "My baby! Please take care of my baby!" She bent at the waist, with a moan and a wail, sobbing progressively louder until she seemed hysterical.

"Shut up!" her captor demanded. When she began to shake uncontrollably, he unleashed a string of threats so vile, Derek considered covering the infant's ears.

"Please," she wailed, unstoppable now, a total distraction. "Protect my baby!"

Blaze and the officer moved closer as she seemed to lose her ever-loving mind.

"Stop crying! Stand up!" the man screamed, then,

noticing the distance law enforcement had gained, he released his grip on her center.

Allison propelled herself forward before his arm was completely away from her waist. He swung an open hand at her head, in an attempt to grab her hair, but Allison was already picking herself up from the muddy ground and launching back through the trees to safety.

Human shield gone, the ATV lurched away, while Blaze and the officer gave chase on foot.

Derek raced into the storm to reunite an incredibly brave mother with her child.

Chapter Seven

Allison stepped out of the shower, exhausted from a long cry and what had been the worst day of her life. She towel-dried her skin and hair, then swept a palm across the fogged mirror, revealing her flushed cheeks and puffy eyes. The bruise on her forehead had darkened, and her limbs were sore, from the truck crash and from fighting uselessly against her relentless assailant.

She cast another protective glance at Bonnie, sleeping soundly in the portable crib against the wall. What mattered was that she was safe and physically unharmed.

Allison ran a comb through her hair, working out the tangles as quickly as possible, eager to get back downstairs. She needed to get dinner in the oven and start cleaning up the mess her intruders had made. Cooking and cleaning always brought her clarity. She needed that now more than ever.

Memories of being discovered in the root cellar played in a loop in her mind. She'd tried going over the situation. Looking for where she'd gone wrong or what she could've done differently, to change the final result, but no matter how many times or ways she reran the encounter, the ending was the same. There hadn't been anywhere to hide. No vehicle to escape in. And the root cellar was the best hiding spot in the house. She was small and scared, and had been attempting to protect her baby. There was only one ugly bottom line. Allison had been trapped and helpless.

And she hated it.

Her chin lifted in defiance, her mind uncomfortably numb as she pulled on an oversize T-shirt and pair of black leggings. The soft cotton material clung to her damp skin as she hurried to join Derek, who was presumably still fixing her door and replacing the locks.

"One more move," she whispered to her sleeping baby. "Then I promise to leave you in one place for the rest of the night."

Allison opened the bathroom door, then pulled the crib into the small upstairs hallway.

Clark waited at the top of the stairs, long tail flopping lazily.

The scent of lemons and a muffled whirring of a power tool rose to meet her from the floor below.

She checked the bedrooms for signs of an intruder, then tested the window locks before depositing Bonnie into her crib in the nursery. She turned on the monitor and carried the receiver with her as she returned to the bathroom to gather her towels and dirty clothes.

Her legs wobbled as she followed Clark toward the kitchen. The pain in her right knee had subsided following the crash, but she suspected it would be tender to touch for days. A nasty bruise had already formed.

Clark and Derek had stayed by her side while local law enforcement canvassed the forest behind her home in search of the ATVs and their riders. The second man had taken off at the sound of sirens, leaving her assailant to drag her along on his own. But her protector and furry sidekick had stuck close to her as she'd given both verbal and written statements. Afterward, Derek had offered her water, aspirin and rest. He was always close by, but never in her personal space. Protective and attentive without pushing her boundaries. All things she'd needed today more than ever. And appreciated more than she could say.

When she'd announced her need for a shower, Derek had hauled a toolbox in from his truck and gotten busy fixing her busted door. But before all of that, he'd protected Bonnie when Allison had abandoned her. For that alone, Allison owed Derek everything.

She stilled on her bottom step, surprised to find a handsome sandy-haired man emptying her trash in a completely cleaned kitchen.

He froze at the sight of her, then saluted in greeting. "I'm Cruz," he said, gaze shifting toward the front room, where the soft whirring of a power tool continued. "Winchester," he added. "Derek's cousin. His partner at the PI firm. Blaze got another call, so I dropped by to pick up where he left off, and bring Derek a go-bag from the office. Change of clothes and whatnot." He scratched behind one ear, looking wildly uncomfortable. "I probably should've made sure it was okay with you first."

Allison smiled despite herself and the awful day. Were all the Winchesters this handsome and helpful? She'd met four of them so far. How many more could there really be? "Thank you for coming," she said. "I appreciate everything you and your family has done for me today. I wish there was something I could do to repay you."

The whirring stopped, and Clark moseyed into the front room.

Derek appeared a moment later. "Looking good," he said, scanning the room before noticing Allison. A wide smile spread across his face as he took her in.

The expression sent a wave of heat through Allison's limbs.

"How was the shower?" he asked.

"Good." She wound her arms around the little ball of dirty laundry against her middle, hoping she'd properly tucked her bra and panties inside the clothes and towel, and hadn't been showing them off to poor Cruz this entire time.

"Are you feeling okay?" Derek asked, probably noticing her flushed cheeks. "Have you eaten? I can make you something."

Cruz's brow wrinkled as he watched the exchange. "Why don't I just run out and pick something up? I can drop it off to you guys on my way home." He tied the trash bag, then marched through the back door with it before she could respond.

"Sorry. That's Cruz," Derek said. "I didn't hear you come downstairs, or I would've introduced you."

"It's okay." Allison fidgeted, still wondering at the strange chemistry working between them. Too many emotions in one day, she supposed. "The kitchen looks great." Everything did.

She moved through the room, baffled by the view of each adjacent space. "How long was I in the shower? Did you clean the whole house?"

"That was mostly Cruz," Derek said. "He came to straighten up while I replaced your doorknob and added a dead bolt. I reinforced the jamb while I was at it."

She turned to the back door, where Cruz had disappeared. The man who'd taken out her trash looked more like the quarterback in a football movie than a man who'd willingly clean her house. Especially so impressively. "You've both done too much. I can take over from here. And as for food, I'd planned to make you dinner before…everything happened. I'd still like to, if you don't mind. Cooking takes my mind off things, and I could use a little of that right now."

Derek's lips pulled into a slow, lazy smile. "You were going to cook for me?"

"I was going to surprise you when you got back from picking up Clark," she admitted, moving toward the stacked washer and dryer in the hallway. "Seemed like the hospitable thing to do."

He crossed his arms and leaned against the archway between rooms. "Is that right?"

"Yes."

The back door opened, and Cruz strode inside. He grabbed an empty trash bag from beneath the kitchen sink, then lined her receptacle with it. "So what's for dinner?" he asked, clasping his hands together. "I'm glad to pick it up."

"I'm going to cook," Allison said. "It'll take about an hour. Is that too long?" She looked to Derek for a response.

He shook his head. "An hour sounds great."

"All right," Cruz said, washing his hands at the sink. "Offer stands if you change your mind."

"Are you leaving?" Allison asked. She opened a pair of folding doors in the hallway, then dropped her laundry into the washing machine hidden inside.

Cruz nodded in confirmation, then clapped his cousin on the shoulder as he passed. "Need anything else, call."

"Yeah." Derek shook his hand.

Allison started the laundry, then went to see out the other Winchester. "Thank you," she called after him, wishing there was more she could do. He was a complete stranger, and he'd cleaned her house. Just because it needed doing. "It was really nice of him to come over and help," Allison said, locking the door. "He doesn't even know me."

"Well, we're family," Derek said. "And it was the right thing to do."

Allison returned to the kitchen, then grabbed the recipe box to start dinner, pointedly ignoring the chemistry that had returned full force in Cruz's absence.

Derek followed her to the counter. "What are you making? And how can I help?"

She laughed. "Chicken-fried steak and mashed potatoes." She dared a look in his direction to check his expression, and he grinned. "Why don't you have a seat? You've done too much already."

Derek sat obediently, then watched intently as she worked.

An hour later, she took the seat across from him at the small kitchen table, and settled in for a hot, home-cooked meal her grandma would've been proud of.

Clark snored near the back door.

"This looks fantastic," Derek said, digging into the meal before him.

"Thanks. I used family recipes. Grandma's for the steak. Mom's for the potatoes."

His eyebrows rose. "Does your mom live nearby?"

"No." Allison forced a tight smile. "She and Dad moved to Florida a few years back. That was when I came to live with Grandma."

"Was she ill?" he asked. "How old were you?"

"I was barely nineteen. I'd just graduated high school and enrolled in a few college courses when Dad retired." She took a bite of the steak and sighed. *Perfect once again.* "Grandma was doing great at the time, and she was really kind to let me stay."

"Nineteen," Derek said, a bit wistfully, as if that age had been a lifetime ago for him. "And you didn't want to move to Florida?"

"I like it here," she said. "But I wasn't in a financial position to stand on my own then. Turns out that working with preschoolers at the day care isn't a high-paying career opportunity." She grinned. "I wasn't thinking about money when I fell in love with the job. I'd finished three of the four years I needed to finish my degree when Grandma's health took a turn. I figured it was a sign, so I focused on her instead of me. Then Bonnie came along." She bit her lip, willing her babbling tongue to stop. "Sorry, I talk too much when I'm nervous."

Derek's brow furrowed, and he leaned forward in his seat. "I make you nervous?"

She lowered her gaze to her plate, unwilling to let him see the truth in her eyes. Derek Winchester made her very nervous, in a number of wildly inappropriate ways. "How did you become a private investigator? That's kind of an unusual line of work around here."

He watched her for a long beat before responding. "I guess that's why I ended up doing it. I spent eight years in the military, nearly half of those overseas. I came home and tried one or two more traditional kinds of things, but they didn't work out." He gave a mischievous smile. "So here I am."

"What kinds of things did you try?" she said. What did Derek think was a normal job? What had he picked? And why hadn't he liked it?

Derek lifted, then dropped one shoulder. "I'd always liked horses, so I competed at a few rodeos for money, but like most cowboys, eventually, I got hurt. I reevaluated my life, and consider law enforcement, because my family loves it so much. I had a bad experience with that early on, and knew it wasn't for me. I have a lot of respect for my brothers. Law enforcement isn't an easy path. Then I realized Blaze and Lucas called on private investigators for legwork all the time. It was stuff I could do. So why not ask them to call me instead?"

"I like that," she said, wishing she could ask about his bad experience, but not wanting to overstep. Derek didn't seem like the type to open up to strangers, so she had to appreciate whatever he was willing to offer. For now. "Do you still ride?"

"As often as I can."

She took another bite of her dinner, and tried to reel in her quickly devolving thoughts. This man had been kind enough to save her and protect her baby. It was fundamentally wrong for her to ogle him and indulge her suddenly specific cowboy fantasies.

He cocked an eyebrow, probably reading her thoughts, and she traded her fork for the glass of ice water before her. "You okay?"

"Mmm-hmm." She set down the glass and refocused. "So who do you think is behind all this?" she asked, pulling a quick and desperate subject change.

"I don't know. Anything's possible. Blaze is reviewing all the recent missing-person reports to see if anyone matches the weight estimates from the footprints at Mason's place. He'll keep us in the loop as things progress."

Allison nodded, glad to know authorities were still looking for the woman, not just the men.

"Blaze will figure this out," Derek said. "He's the

best at his job, and this case is personal. I haven't seen him this motivated in a while. Justice will be served. You can bank on that."

She raised her eyes carefully to Derek and steeled her nerves. "I want to help. I saw both of their faces, and I'd like to go to the police department tomorrow morning. Maybe Blaze will let me look through mug shots in the criminal database."

Derek finished his last bite of dinner without speaking, then wiped his mouth and set aside his napkin.

She balled her hands into fists beneath the table. Her truck was in the shop, and she needed him to agree to this. She needed him to drive her.

"All right."

"Thank you." Her tension bled away, and she returned to her meal with a smile.

"I have something to ask in return."

Her limbs tightened. "What?"

"Let me stay here a few days," he said. "Until Blaze is sure it's safe for you to be alone, or until your truck's fixed, at least."

A few days? Living with Derek? Her mind perked with possibilities. Her heart swelled with gratitude. She'd planned to ask for just one night, but this was so much better. "You don't have to do that," she said, trying to be polite, when she wanted to throw her arms around his neck. "I'm sure you have a life to get back to, and you've already done so much."

"You could've been killed the last time I left," he

said, expression grim. "I won't make that mistake twice. Mason would never forgive me."

Heat fanned across her cheeks. His words were a firm reminder of their situation. Fantasies aside, Derek was here out of obligation to a mutual friend. Any imagined connection she felt between them was nothing more than her loneliness and a day of heightened emotions. "Fine."

"Fine," he echoed, then extended a hand over the table for her to shake.

She slid her palm against his and her lips parted as the fireworks began.

Something flashed in his dark eyes, and she wondered if he'd felt it, too.

She pulled her hand away, having obviously learned nothing from Bonnie's dad. "I should get some sleep," she said, abruptly rising. "Leave all this. I'll handle it in the morning." She motioned absently to the remaining meal and dishes that needed to be washed. "I'm going to toss my laundry into the dryer, then run upstairs to get you a blanket and pillow for the couch."

She stopped before reaching the small closet with her washer and dryer. A scrap of paper caught her eye on the floor by her toes. She crouched to retrieve it and a memory flickered through her hazy mind. This was the paper she'd found inside the fence around Mason's chicken coop.

The gentle rattling of dishes barely registered as she stared at the faded, water-smeared script. Letters. Numbers. None of it with any apparent meaning.

And it wasn't Mason's handwriting. She'd thought it was trash this morning. Could it be something more?

Could it have belonged to one of the killers?

She moved back to the kitchen, mind racing, then smiled when Derek came into view washing dishes. "I said to leave that alone. For a man with eight years in the military, you don't follow orders very well."

He dried his hands on a towel across his shoulder and grinned. "I get that a lot."

Allison rolled her eyes as she moved closer. "I picked this up outside Mason's house this morning. I guess it fell out of my pocket when I put my clothes in the washer." She extended one hand, the paper between her fingertips. "It doesn't mean anything to me, but maybe it's relevant to the case?" It was a shot in the dark, but she was willing to turn over every stone in Kentucky if it meant finding the men who'd hurt Mason and forced her to abandon her baby.

He took the paper from her fingers slowly. "I'll take a look," he said. "We can give it to Blaze in the morning."

Allison excused herself to get Derek that blanket and pillow.

For the first time in far too long, hope wiggled in her chest. She'd lost her parents to their retirement, her boyfriend to his dreams, which didn't include an unexpected family, and her grandmother to illness. But just maybe she could help find justice for Mason. And maybe the poor woman he'd tried to help would be saved after all.

Chapter Eight

Unable to find any significant measure of sleep, despite her complete fatigue, Allison was up before the sun. She cleaned her room, researched police procedures for a murder investigation, then worked her long hair into two French braids. Next, she applied a little mascara, then sulked in front of her closet and the limited amount of nonmaternity clothing she could fit into.

Bonnie stretched in her portable playpen, and Allison hurried across the room to see her baby's little cherub face. She hadn't been able to rest knowing Bonnie was alone in the nursery across the hall, and the men who'd separated them earlier were still on the loose. So she'd moved her baby one more time, and relaxed a tiny fraction afterward.

"Good morning, my sweet princess," she whispered, lifting Bonnie from the little bed. "I missed you while you were sleeping. I hope you had wonderful happy dreams." She nuzzled her baby close and pressed a row of gentle kisses across her face. "I'll bet you're ready for a pretty outfit and a big breakfast."

Allison carried Bonnie back to the nursery and selected a comfy outfit for her day. A pale pink bodysuit with white leggings that hugged every dimpled inch of her tiny butterball body. Her socks were printed to look like ballet slippers, crisscrossing up her chubby baby calves. One quick diaper change and stretchy headband selection later, and the Hill women were ready for breakfast.

Allison descended the stairs on her tiptoes, with Bonnie snuggled into her sling.

The newly risen sun cast a warm amber-and-apricot glow over the world, illuminating dew on grass outside the windows and flooding her kitchen with light.

Allison pulled a baby bottle and nipple from the insanely organized cupboard, then added scoops of formula and water. She shook the bottle as she scanned the rooms for signs of Clark. Surely he had to go outside by now.

She craned her neck for a look into the living room, hoping Derek had found at least a little rest on her couch. But he was gone, the blanket neatly folded and stacked on his pillow.

The back door opened, and she nearly leaped out of her skin.

"Morning," Derek said, bare-chested and dragging a T-shirt across his brow like a towel. "I didn't wake you, did I?"

"No." She'd been up for hours, but hadn't felt truly awake until this moment.

Clark lumbered in on Derek's heels, big tail flapping. He drank most of the water from his bowl, sloshing the rest over her clean linoleum, then collapsed where he'd stood.

"I feel you, old man," Derek said, stooping briefly to scratch Clark's head and stomach.

Allison pressed her lips together, forcibly dragging her attention away from the bead of sweat traveling between the planes of Derek's lean, muscled chest. Down the flat, narrow V of his torso and into the dark trail of hair that vanished beneath the waistband of his basketball shorts.

He fanned the T-shirt out as he stood, threading ropey muscled arms into the sleeves, then pulling the material over his head.

She suppressed a disappointed groan as she shook the baby bottle, mixing the formula and water. "I've been up awhile," she said. "I'm surprised I didn't hear you leave."

He shrugged. "Clark needed to go out, and I wanted to get a good look at your property beyond the yard. How many acres do you have here?"

"Eight."

He nodded, helping himself to a bottle of water in the refrigerator. "I worried the guys on the ATVs were getting here by way of the river, but your access is awful. I ran along the edge for a while, but I don't think they got here by river. They're either coming from land with the ATV's or getting off the water somewhere else, then riding the rest of the way."

That was true. Her property butted up to the river, but there wasn't an access point. Just a pretty steep drop-off, about half a mile through the woods with water below. The hill was covered in thorns and brush. Nothing like Mason's place, which had level ground and a nice dock.

"How far did you run?" she asked, contemplating his sweat-dampened hair and Clark's utter fatigue.

"Not quite down to Mason's and back, but I wasn't gone more than twenty minutes, and I wouldn't have left at all if I thought there was any chance you were in danger."

He'd run close to two miles in twenty minutes. The farthest she ran these days was through the local Piggly Wiggly for baby wipes. And that was exhausting.

She offered the bottle to Bonnie, who greedily accepted. "Did you see anything I should be concerned about?"

Derek finished the water, then recapped the bottle before setting it in a box Cruz had designated for recycling. "It's a clean slate out there. ATV tracks were washed away by the storm, but it can't be a coincidence that I left to get Clark yesterday, and the same two guys you'd seen at Mason's showed up in that thirty- or forty-minute window."

"You think they followed me?" Allison asked. "Well, that figures. Here I am thinking it'll take forever to access a license-plate database and track my vehicle to my home. Meanwhile, the bad guys just go the old-fashioned route and follow me home." She laughed humorlessly, then rolled her eyes for effect.

Derek gripped the back of his neck. "It's possible they were watching the crime scene. Maybe keeping tabs on our progress toward their identification, then I showed up, so they knew you were alone. Hard to let a perfect opportunity go."

"Risky, though," she said. "Waiting around to see if they were going to be caught instead of running. Why would they do that?"

Derek leaned against the counter, stretching long legs before him and crossing his feet at the ankles. "That was my next question, too."

"Got any answers?" she asked, moving in beside him to put on some coffee. She needed to be alert when she arrived at the police station. Identifying either ATV rider would be a great step toward naming and locating them both.

"Only one," he said, lifting a small sandwich baggie from the napkin holder on the table. Inside was the scrap of paper she'd found in Mason's chicken coop.

"You think those notations mean something to them?"

He nodded. "And I think they want this back."

Allison poured a mug of coffee, considering how important the little rain-smeared scrap could be. And why. "What do you think the letters and numbers mean?"

"Not sure," he said. "I sent a photo of the paper to Blaze last night, and he said he'd work on it." Derek stepped unexpectedly closer to Allison, eyes on Bonnie as she enjoyed her bottle. "How's she doing?" he asked.

Her big blue eyes rose to meet his curious gaze. Her features were rapt with intensity, as always, taking in unthinkable amounts of information and learning a million tiny new things every second.

"She seems completely fine. She slept well. Her mood and appetite are good." Pride welled in Allison's heart as she spoke, beating out the unbearable mommy guilt that had plagued her all night. "I did some research online that suggests she's too young for any of this trauma to leave any lasting marks on her psyche, assuming I don't go insane from it all. If she's raised by an anxious, paranoid nut, that will be another story."

Derek stepped back, returning his attention to Allison. "I don't think you have to worry about that. You're stronger than you think."

"Ha." She spoke the word. "You are wrong, sir. I am a complete mess. And her only role model. She'll look to me for guidance, strength, love, compassion, or whatever else her sweet little self needs. Some days I'm more aware than others of how unfair that is to her."

Derek's eyes narrowed, and Allison's throat clogged.

"I'm sorry," she said. "I don't know why I said that." She set down the mug and released a shaky breath before moving Bonnie and her bottle to a bouncy seat on the floor.

Clark dragged up his big body, moved four feet to Bonnie's chair, then lied down again, head on his paws, and eyes on Bonnie.

"They're old friends," Allison said, suddenly missing Mason more than she could stand.

An expression of confliction crossed Derek's

handsome face, then he opened his arms, and Allison fell in easily.

She pressed her cheek to his shirt, eyes stinging and throat burning as she accepted the embrace. "Thank you," she whispered. Her broken, grieving heart had needed this more than she'd known.

His broad hands pressed against her back, strong arms cocooning her in a protective embrace.

She considered pulling away after a brief moment, determined not to be as needy as she felt, but his cheek came down against her head, and she thought that maybe he needed the contact, too.

"No one has hugged me in a year," she said, offering him honesty in return for all he'd done for her. "Not since Grandma died, the funeral ended and my family went back to Florida. Mason was an incredible support, but he was more of a side-hug, pat-on-the-back guy." Another reminder that she was absolutely all that Bonnie had in this world, and she had to be enough. Whether she felt like it or not.

DEREK CARRIED BONNIE'S little spaceship of a car seat to his truck and snapped it into place on the base. Allison had put the other seat out with the trash, taking time to write on it in permanent marker. Do Not Use. Has Been in a Crash. Apparently, she feared someone might stop along the roadside and pick it up.

Bonnie sucked on her pudgy fingers and drooled on the bib Allison had fastened around her neck. She smiled at Derek, and he smiled back. It was easy to see why parents went so insane over their babies. He'd only met this kid yesterday and was already unintentionally and inexplicably attached. How could he not be? She was too tiny to defend herself from anything. Her hand-eye coordination was terrible. Her only defense were those gummy smiles and big doe eyes.

Allison's gaze snapped him from the silly chain of thoughts and put him back in the moment.

"Ready?" he asked, climbing behind the wheel and pulling carefully onto the road. He'd taken the extra time to unhitch and remove the horse trailer while Allison and Bonnie gathered everything they needed for the outing. It took up too much space outside the little farmhouse, but he couldn't afford to be hindered by it any longer. Not if there was a chance he might be chased by whoever had hurt Mason and come for Allison.

"Thanks for taking me today," she said, hands fidgeting in her lap. "Sorry you had to leave your trailer. Nowhere to park with it near the police station?" she asked.

"Nowhere close," he said, going with that, also accurate, point of reason.

He stole a glance at her faded Patsy Cline T-shirt and ripped jeans with sneakers. Long blond braids hung over her shoulders, and she'd pulled a ball cap on to shade her eyes from the sun. Probably also to cover the bruise she tried and failed to disguise with a flutter of pale bangs. Injury aside, she looked like every girl-next-door fantasy he'd ever had. Allison Hill was a single mom in need of a protector, not a lover, and he needed to remember that.

She and her little girl deserved someone who could stay in their lives for the long haul and make it better. They deserved more than he could offer, and if he hadn't known it before, he had unequivocally gotten the message when she told him she hadn't been hugged in a year.

How was that even possible?

Who had held her through the loss or rejection of her baby's father? Derek didn't know the specifics, but surely, however he'd exited the scene, it had been painful for her. And what? She'd gotten through it on her own? Pregnant and alone. No best friend? No siblings or cousins? A coworker she spent time with, at least?

The same surge of unintentional thoughts about Allison rose in his cluttered mind. He saw her carrying Bonnie onto the deck at his folks' house. Hugging his parents, his siblings and their significant others. He saw Allison's heart and life full and happy, irrevocably twined with his, but he pushed away the image. He wasn't sure what to do with these thoughts, or why his usually sharp mind had chosen now, in the middle of a murder investigation, to go on the fritz.

But it had. In a big, distracting way.

Allison wasn't alone in his weird daydreams. He saw himself at her side, loaded down with diaper bags and pop-up playpens, lacing her fingers with his as they walked.

"You look angry," she said, breaking the silence at the only red light between her place and town.

He dared a look in her direction, hoping the ridiculous thoughts weren't written on his face. "What happened between you and Bonnie's dad?" he asked, knowing it was rude, but needing her answer more than he needed to be polite.

She averted her gaze in response. "I don't know what you mean."

Derek moved his attention back to the road when the light changed. He needed to let the subject go, but knew he couldn't. "I mean, isn't he usually around? Because it seems to me you might've called him," he said. "Or he should've shown up by now, having gotten word of all this mess, and come straight home to… I don't know. To be here for you. And for his little girl."

She turned her attention to the window at her side. Her hands gripped into fists on her lap.

He'd gone too far, and it showed in her pained expression. The fact that he'd been the one to make her look that way horrified him. "I'm sorry. I shouldn't have pushed. It's none of my business what's going on with you and Bonnie's daddy."

"Bonnie doesn't have a daddy," Allison snapped. "Daddies take their little girls on walks. They hold them and read bedtime stories and tell them how much they love them. I had a boyfriend who left the moment he learned I was pregnant. He has never been anything to Bonnie and he never will be. He didn't even want his name on the birth certificate. I know because I asked when I called him from the hospital, after I'd given birth alone because my folks couldn't make it here from Florida in time. He didn't answer my earlier calls when I went into labor. He's never even seen her."

Derek closed his mouth and wished hard that he'd learn to take his own advice once in a while. He'd unintentionally poked a sore, and Allison had enough immediate problems without him bringing up past ones, too. "Sorry," he said again. "I shouldn't have pried."

She slid her eyes briefly in his direction. "It's fine."

"You've probably heard this before," he said, "but that guy doesn't deserve to know you or your baby. He sounds like the kind of person who'd only drag you down. You should be with someone who does all the things you think a man should do, and about a dozen more you haven't even thought of. There's no bar too high for you and your baby girl."

Her grimace softened, and his heart followed suit. "Thanks," she said. "No one has actually said that to me. I appreciate it."

"If you ever need reminding, give me a call."

He slowed as the police station came into view, then he smiled. "I'm not saying some men aren't cocky pains in the backside. I'm just saying, some of them are worth the trouble."

And for the first time in a long time, he wanted to be one of those.

Chapter Nine

The West Liberty Police Department was a sprawling one-story stone building, surrounded by beautiful landscaping that blended pleasantly into the quaint downtown setting. It was just blocks from a small, but busy, shop-lined and inviting college campus. The Bellemont student body made up half the town's population nine months of the year, and the school was a major source of local jobs and income. So the police in West Liberty were well-cared for, and by the looks of their station, maybe even a little spoiled.

Allison smiled. Bellemont was exactly the kind of place she'd feel safe sending Bonnie one day. Derek had spoken proudly of his brothers' positions on the local force over dinner. He'd said the chief made it known that keeping the peace and maintaining the small-town status quo was imperative for keeping their jobs, and that getting a spot at the West Liberty PD was a testament to the reputation, behavior and personal record of each officer and detective.

She'd liked getting a peek at that side of Derek. Something about a proud big brother made her happy. People always talked about how much they fought with their siblings, but the Winchesters were close, the way she thought families were supposed to be. It made sense that they'd live and work in a perfect little town. Their sheer existence felt a little like something from a storybook to Allison, especially when compared to her reality.

She watched the pretty shops pass by. The couples holding hands. People pushing strollers. Walking dogs. "I really like this town," she said, as much to herself as to Derek. It was too bad murderous criminals were putting their ugly marks all over it.

Derek looked her way. "It's usually a good place to be. What was your old town like?"

"Smaller than this, and sad. We had a church and a post office. That's it. No work. No stoplight. It was a socioeconomic nightmare. Kids were bussed over an hour to school, and there weren't any jobs, so depression, crime and drug abuse were high. No police or local hospital."

Derek parked the truck in the lot marked for visitors, then frowned. "That does sound sad," he admitted. "Frustrating for sure. For everyone."

"Pretty much." She climbed down from the cab, thankful she'd been able to leave when so many people she'd grown up with likely never would. "West Liberty seems perfect. It has everything anyone could need without all the fuss of a big city. Plenty of space to breathe and be free, without the trouble of a thirty-minute drive just to get gas."

Derek laughed. "We do have our share of gas stations."

She circled the truck, then stopped at his side and waited as he unfastened Bonnie and lifted her from her car seat. Big hands curled around Bonnie's middle on either side. "You should hold her against you," she said softly, unsure if she was being presumptuous by assuming he had any interest in holding her baby correctly. "Her neck muscles are still developing."

He pulled Bonnie to his chest, resting her head against him while Allison dropped the loop of fabric she used to carry Bonnie over her shoulder. He rearranged his hold, adjusting one broad forearm beneath her for support. Then he raised his eyes and eyebrows to Allison.

"Yeah." She nodded. "That's perfect."

Bonnie made a vibrating raspberry sound and spit bubbles pooled at the corners of her mouth. When Derek turned his face to her, she gave him a wide toothless grin.

"I can take her." Allison reached for her baby, dabbing her little lips with the bib before tucking her into the sling. It was strange to see someone else holding her baby, and a mass of feelings crashed and collided in her core. Appreciation. Care. Fear. Panic. "We should probably take her seat, too. She gets fussy if I sit too long."

Derek popped the empty seat away from the base, then led the way to the check-in desk inside the lobby.

"Hey, Derek," the young woman behind the counter said upon their approach. "Go on back."

He changed directions with a smile and lift of his hand, moving toward a metal door as it emitted a soft buzz. He held the door for Allison to pass into a wide interior hall.

The walls were painted a soft gray and lined with photos and awards won by local officers and the department. The air was cool and scented with black coffee.

Derek stopped at the door with Blaze's name on it. Another, similar-looking man was already inside speaking with the detective. "Hey," Derek said, strolling directly inside. He shook hands with each man, then motioned Allison forward from where she lingered at the threshold. "Blaze, you remember Allison. Lucas, I'm sure you've heard all about her by now. Allison—" he turned to her, with a small sweeping motion of one hand "—this is my other little brother, Lucas. He's also a detective here. SVU, not homicide."

Allison lifted one hand hip-high, feeling incredibly small in the face of three towering Winchesters.

Lucas offered her his hand. "Nice to finally meet you." His gaze drifted over Bonnie, then flipped to Derek and the car seat as he released Allison's fingers. "I like this look on you."

Allison smiled. Derek looked adorable. All muscles and attitude with a polka-dotted bag over one shoulder and a bulbous pink-and-gray car seat dangling from the opposite hand.

She'd forgotten to grab the bag from the truck, but he hadn't said a word. He'd simply brought it along.

Her heart swelled with appreciation, and she smiled more brightly at the clearly baffled Winchester before her. "Nice to meet you, too, Lucas. This is Bonnie. She and I are hoping to take a look at some mug shots today."

"Right," he said, clapping his hands once, then stepping out of the way. "I guess I'll let y'all get to it then. Gwen's on her way in with lunch. She always brings enough for anyone who're interested. We eat in the courtyard outside, if you want to join us."

"That sounds nice," Allison answered, a little overeager.

Derek grinned. "We'd love to. Let us know when she gets here."

Blaze motioned Allison to one of the guest chairs in front of his desk. A laptop had been set up before it. "I've already logged in to the database. You can dig in whenever you're ready."

She took a seat, then kissed Bonnie before she got to work scanning photographs.

Beside her, Derek and Blaze skipped the pleasantries and dove into shoptalk.

"So far, preliminary information is being processed, and most of our assumptions were confirmed. The blood found in Mason's kitchen wasn't his. Some casts made from the footprints outside his home were a match for the size and tread on prints found outside Allison's home. However, there were also a batch of smaller, size-eight boot prints on Mason's property that weren't at Allison's."

"Any idea where the ATVs are coming from?"

Derek asked. "I ran along the river today, but didn't see a good place for them to cross until I reached the edge of Mason's land."

"Both sets of ATV tracks ran along the river, in the direction of Mason's home, before disappearing near an access road mostly used by the county."

Derek shifted his weight, stewing at Allison's side. "Any luck with the missing-persons flyers?"

"Maybe." Blaze moved to his chair, and Derek took the other visitor's seat, dropping the diaper bag at his feet. "Three women match the approximate weight of the woman who left prints at Mason's place. Each woman was slightly heavier than our guesstimate at the time she was reported missing, but they're all close. And they have something else in common. Each of them vanished while running errands in a busy shopping section of her hometown. Three different towns, but all in the last month."

"Serial killer?" Derek asked.

Allison's stomach clenched, then nearly revolted. Her hands froze on the laptop's touchpad as she waited for Blaze's response.

"I don't think so. Their physical appearances vary greatly. If they were taken by the same person, he doesn't seem to have a specific type, beyond blonde. Though, they were all relatively young. Ages nineteen to twenty-four. The fact that they were all shopping at the time they went missing, and were all from river towns, suggests we have a definitive pattern of behavior."

Allison stopped pretending not to eavesdrop. Her

frozen hands began to tremble, and she put them in her lap, kneading them roughly together. "You're talking about human trafficking." She swung her gaze from Blaze to Derek, then back. "That's why Lucas was in here. Because he's SVU."

Derek's lips parted, and his gaze flicked to Blaze. Had Derek already put those details together?

Was she right?

Blaze scratched behind one ear. "It's an avenue we're exploring, but it's only a possibility at this point."

Derek kicked back in his seat, hooking one foot over the opposite knee. "Anything concrete that might lead you in that direction?"

Blaze leaned forward, elbows on the desk between them. "Trace evidence on Mason's flannel shirt revealed DNA from more than one woman. We suspect the hairs transferred from the injured woman when Mason attempted to help her. If she's being held in close quarters with other women, it would go along with what we know about how women and children are moved in trafficking situations."

Allison's arms curled around her daughter, who was cooing contentedly in the sling. Her heart rate climbed and fear clutched at her soul. There were sex traffickers in this town? Two had been in her home? With her daughter? Suddenly, having left Bonnie behind during the attempted abduction was a larger blessing than she'd imagined.

"The lab is comparing the hairs and blood type with the three missing women I flagged. One of my guys is pulling similar files from the last six months," Blaze said.

Allison's ears rang as she continued to listen to the men rehashing theories and making plans to collect more evidence. Eventually, she found a man in the database who looked a little like the one who'd had a hold of her. He had a long beard and bald head in the photo, but he'd been clean-shaven with casual, floppy hair when he'd dragged her away from her home. The photo was taken six years ago, but the eyes were the same—a little too cool for a mug shot, too detached for the circumstance. A fifth arrest for domestic violence.

Lucas and a tall woman with red curly hair appeared in the doorway as Allison turned to tell Blaze about the image. Lucas introduced the woman as his fiancée, Gwen, then led them all to the courtyard outside. Allison shared her suspicions about the man in the mug shot on their way. "Redmon Firth. Thirty-two. From Cincinnati, Ohio."

Blaze sent off a text and patted her shoulder. "Nice work."

The police station formed a large U shape around a courtyard. Outlined in parking lots and a chain-link fence, the building's small parklike center, with picnic benches, young trees and clusters of flowers, didn't surprise Allison at all. A birdhouse on a pole had been painted blue and resembled a cartoon police station, while whirligigs swung their arms near the glass employee entrance.

Cameras on the roofline covered the courtyard,

and a mechanical gate allowed only cruisers and official vehicles to park in the visible lot. The space felt a little like a sanctuary.

Allison took a seat beside Derek at the table, where Gwen unpacked an honest-to-goodness picnic basket, complete with a tablecloth, cups, silverware and plates. She'd brought three croissant sandwich options. Ham and cheese, chicken salad or turkey and swiss. Plastic bowls of fruit. Tossed salad. And freshly baked brownies, transported in a thermal carrier to keep them warm.

"I hope you'll find something you like," Gwen said. "I never know what to bring, so I try to make a little of everything."

"This is amazing," Allison said, touched at her thoughtfulness, and moved by her own inclusion in the little group. It'd been a long time since she'd been asked to share a meal with anyone.

The men helped themselves, while Gwen smiled and chatted along, completely at ease.

This is what family looks like, Allison realized. She'd had something like it with her parents when she was small, though the conversations were more tense, the smiles and laughter nonexistent. She'd had happier meals with her grandma for a little while, then with Mason, and she suddenly missed them deeply. This family before her wasn't hers to claim, but she ate up the sweet moments, anyway. She'd keep them on hand to enjoy later, when the danger had passed, and she and Bonnie were alone once more, figuring life out on their own.

Lucas set aside his second sandwich to check his phone. Blaze wiped his mouth on a napkin, then did the same.

"What?" Derek asked, nearly in unison with Gwen, who smiled at him.

Lucas kissed her forehead, already pushing onto his feet. "The prison warden's got something to share. He wants me on a video conference with the chief."

Blaze stood, collecting his trash. "I'm coming," he called after his brother. "Everything was fantastic, as always, Gwen, thank you. You make me want to go home and cook for Maisy tonight. If either of us can stay awake long enough to eat."

"You know Luke and I will babysit anytime," she said. "The two of you can do whatever you want for as long as you need."

"We're going to take you up on that," he said, "especially if Lucas changes the diapers."

"Deal," she agreed.

Derek looked from his retreating brothers to Allison.

"Go," she said. "Tell me everything when you get back."

His jaw set, then he was on his feet in an instant. He leaned in, as if he might kiss her head, the way Lucas had kissed Gwen. He stopped short, color draining from his face, and straightened instead. "Enjoy the rest of your meal, ladies."

"Uh…" Gwen said, as the three Winchesters darted back into the building. "Was he about to kiss you? Do you two do that?"

"No," Allison said. "Never." Her cheeks flamed hot as she turned to look at the now closed door, all traces of the men gone. "I'm not sure what that was about."

"Interesting," Gwen said. She popped a grape into her mouth and smiled.

"He volunteered to protect Bonnie and me until the men who hurt Mason and broke into my home are caught," Allison said. "Actually," she amended, "Blaze told him to do it, and he just went along."

Gwen shook her head, selecting another grape. "Derek Winchester doesn't do anything he doesn't want to do. And I never thought I'd see the day he willingly carried a polka-dotted diaper bag through a police station. How'd you manage that?"

Allison smiled, refocusing on her meal. "I forgot it in the truck. He grabbed it and carried it inside." Then again from Blaze's office to the courtyard. "Have you known these guys long?"

"Years," Gwen said. "I started dating Luke in college, and I was close to his family until our breakup. That's a long story." Something dark flashed in her eyes, and Allison averted her gaze, not wanting to pry. "When I came back into the picture," Gwen continued, a little more quietly, "Luke and I fell right into step, as if eight years hadn't passed. It's like that with all of them. The whole Winchester crew. They're all just glad to meet folks and help however they can."

Allison's thoughts snagged on the description. "The whole crew? Are there a lot of them?"

"Winchesters?" Gwen laughed. "Yeah. I'm pretty sure they're at least loosely related to half the country. And they know everyone else."

Allison marveled. "What must that be like?"

"Crazy," Gwen answered. "Absolutely bonkers, but I have a feeling you'll see for yourself soon, so I'll leave it at that." She wiped her hands and pointed to Bonnie, who'd begun to fuss in the car seat, where she was gnawing on a rattle. "May I?"

"Sure." Allison freed her daughter from the harness, then passed Bonnie to her new friend. "I'll make her a bottle. She's probably ready by now."

Allison enjoyed the rest of her meal, while Gwen fed Bonnie and filled her in on all the best places to visit in town and told stories about her time with Lucas at Bellemont College. She even invited Allison out for lunch as soon as things were safe.

Gwen turned Bonnie against her chest and patted her back gently, the bottle empty.

The sound that followed made both women freeze briefly.

Bonnie's spit-up appeared on Gwen's pretty green blouse and in her curly red hair.

"Oh!" Allison jumped. "I am so sorry. That hardly ever happens." She pulled Bonnie away and held her carefully as she searched one-handed through the diaper bag Derek had left behind. "I have baby wipes, but you're going to need cold water to save that blouse."

"It's no problem," Gwen said, standing quickly and still smiling. "It's just a blouse. I'd gladly pay double to hold that little angel again. Just the same, I'm going to see what I can do about my hair," she said, tilting her head to keep the wet curls away from her face. "I'll be right back, and I'll send Derek out if I see him." She hurried toward the door.

Allison wiped Bonnie's face, then swapped her bib for a new one and laughed nervously. "You sure know how to add a little excitement to things." She had no idea if formula came out of silk, but she certainly hoped so. "How about you play with your rattle again while Mommy cleans up for Ms. Gwen?"

With Bonnie safely returned to the car seat, Allison quickly repacked the picnic basket to take inside. She swiveled Bonnie's car seat to face the trash bin across the grassy courtyard and smiled. "I'll toss this out, then we'll go check on Gwen. How does that sound?"

Allison speed-walked to the receptacle several yards away, then spun back the moment her hands were empty.

The temperature of the charming outdoor space seemed to drop as the hairs on her arms rose, and something hard pressed suddenly against her spine. Something that felt distinctly like the barrel of a gun. She'd barely processed the sensation and change in the atmosphere, before a low voice spoke into her ear. "Turn around slowly and follow me quietly, or I shoot."

Terror locked her limbs and panic seized her chest. She recognized his voice, his scent, his grip.

The man who'd dragged her from her home had found her. Again.

Her baby's face crumbled into the expression she made before screaming.

"Why are you doing this?" she asked, voice quivering. "This is the police station. There are cameras. Anything you do will only make things worse."

He sank his fingers into her hair and curled them. "Because the boss wants you now, and if I come back empty-handed, I'll end up like that old man. I can't show my face again without you."

Bonnie's scream cracked through the air like lightning, and the man behind Allison tensed.

"You don't have to do this, Redmon," she whispered, testing the name she'd linked to him in the criminal database. "You can run. Leave whoever is making you do this. Or turn him in."

Bonnie continued to wail, and Allison's assailant shifted behind her.

He crouched suddenly, then grabbed her around the middle and lifted her feet from the ground. Whatever had been pressed against her spine was gone.

And Allison began to fight.

She thrashed and screamed, intentionally amping up her baby's distress, uniting their cries as she kicked at the man's shins and swung her elbows against his ribs.

Redmon wrestled and cussed. How bad was the man he worked for that this was worth coming to the police station to keep him happy? "Stop," he groaned. "Stop, or I'll come back for your daughter."

Allison froze and shut her mouth.

The door to the courtyard burst open, and Derek launched himself toward them, already moving at full speed.

Redmon twisted at his waist, planting both feet, and tilted Allison with him before throwing her with a feral grunt.

She screamed as her body collided hard with Derek's a moment before they landed like two football players, bouncing against the rough stone of the courtyard pathway. Air pressed from Allison's lungs on the impact, choking her breaths and sending spots through her vision.

Her world went black to the sounds of Bonnie's screams.

Chapter Ten

Derek paced the small conference room where Isaac examined Allison. He'd never been so happy to see his cousin's face. Isaac had appeared in the courtyard amid the cluster of officers when Derek had gathered Allison into his arms, demanding a medic.

Apparently, Gwen had already invited one particular medic to the station for a free homemade lunch, and Isaac was answering her call.

Isaac cleaned and bandaged Allison's cuts and scrapes, making small talk and likely listening for signs of slurred speech or confusion. Her impact with the courtyard walkway had rubbed the skin from her elbows and left bruising along her forearms. Every minor injury was a gift. The alternative being her successful abduction, which wasn't something Derek could live with.

Isaac scanned her eyes with a penlight for the third time, then tucked the device back into his shirt pocket. "I think everything looks good. Your loss of consciousness was brief, and I'm not seeing any indications of a head injury. You probably passed out due to the way you landed. Sometimes falling flat on your back will cause a brief lack of oxygen, or an inability to catch your breath. Totally common. Add in the extreme circumstances, racing pulse and elevated blood pressure…" He tipped his head over one shoulder, then the other.

"But I'm fine?" she asked.

"Yeah."

Allison exhaled deeply, relief changing her features, removing the fear.

Derek cringed at the memory. He'd crashed into her, completely shocked by the lunatic's unexpected move. He'd thrown her, as if they were playing games at the local pool and there was water to cushion her fall. What would've happened if Derek was a little slower? He'd taken the brunt of the impact while upright, but Allison had landed hard on her back when they'd hit the ground. And then she'd gone limp.

It had been the second scariest moment of his day. The first being several moments prior, when he'd heard Bonnie scream, then seen some beefed-up nut attempting to drag away Allison.

Derek's temper had exploded. He'd imagined hurting the man in ways he wasn't proud of, and was immeasurably thankful things hadn't come to that.

He scrubbed both palms against his face and unintentionally groaned.

Bonnie made a goofy hiccup sound that made him open his eyes.

He dropped his hands and stared at the smiling

little girl in the car seat, kicking chubby legs and cooing. "Are you laughing at me?"

Isaac approached with a grin. "It's possible. She is a woman."

Allison crouched beside the car seat and unfastened her baby. "Some babies can laugh as early as twelve weeks. Bonnie won't be that old for three more days. She's incredibly advanced. And you're pretty funny."

"I'm not funny," Derek said, frowning at Allison, then Isaac.

Isaac packed up his things. "Not intentionally."

A collection of footfalls sounded outside the door a moment before Blaze, Lucas and Gwen appeared.

"She's just fine," Isaac answered, closing his kit.

The newcomers shared a collective exhale.

"Well?" Derek asked, drawing his brothers' eyes. "What the hell happened out there? This is a police station, right? Full of trained officers. How did a man we're all looking for show up here without being noticed? And where is he now? Because, I would certainly hope you caught him. Right?"

Blaze raised a flat palm to stop his rant.

Allison moved slowly into the space at Derek's side, with Bonnie snuggled to her chest. "He got away," she whispered, correctly reading the detectives' apologetic faces.

Derek's arm slid around her back. To his surprise and satisfaction, she leaned into the touch.

Fire kindled in his chest and limbs. He recalled that she hadn't been held or hugged in more than a year before this week. Now, two men had put their hands on her in as many days. Him, and a killer.

The latter was luckier by the minute that Derek hadn't reached him today.

"We've got the guy on camera circling the station about thirty minutes before he appears in the courtyard," Blaze said. "He probably followed you here from Allison's house. Lunch in the courtyard was a bad move on our part. He used the woods around the rear lot for cover, cut the fence with bolt cutters, then waited for his opportunity to make a move."

Gwen covered her mouth. "And I left you. I'm so sorry."

Lucas pulled Gwen against his side. "Cameras show him making his way to the building before you went inside." His body tensed at the words, and Gwen's hand came up to rest against his middle.

"He had a gun," Allison said softly. "He pressed it to my back before we fought. He needed both hands to lift me."

Derek gritted his teeth against the image. The attacker had planned to take both women. He would've used Gwen against Allison, threatened to hurt her, like he had the baby, and Allison would've caved. The truth of it was both infuriating and heartbreaking. Because Derek would do the same thing in her situation, and because someone so evil could use the good of his victim so easily against her.

"You fought, knowing he had a gun?" Blaze asked.

Gwen looked ill, much like Derek felt. He bit his

tongue against the list of complaints and protests piling there.

Allison nodded. "He said he had to take me to someone, so I assumed that meant alive."

"Who?" the men asked simultaneously.

"He didn't name him," she said, "but I called the man who had me *Redmon*. It's the name I saw on the mug shot, and he didn't correct me."

Blaze crossed his arms and Lucas nodded.

Isaac looked from one brother to the other. "And?"

"That's what pulled us inside," Blaze said. "I flagged the mug shot and got feedback pretty quickly. He has a history of low-level aggressions, fighting, drunk and disorderly, domestic violence. He was just released after a six-month stint about forty-five days ago. We're tracking him now. Looking for places he's stayed, jobs he's had, family or friends he's visited."

Allison made a small, sad sound, then turned beneath Derek's protective arm and rested her forehead against his chest, cocooning her baby between them.

His arms curled protectively over her on instinct. "Something's got to change," he said, flicking his gaze from one brother to the next, then to Isaac, the cousin who'd been raised as closely as any blood sibling could ever be. "I can't take her back to her place if there's any chance he followed us from there."

She lifted her head, rolling away from him once more, and squared her narrow shoulders. "He told me getting caught today would've been better than going back to wherever he's staying without me. If there's an upside, it's that whoever the other guy is, he doesn't want me dead, at least not yet."

"That's good," Blaze said.

"How is that good?" Derek growled.

Isaac smiled congenially and lifted both hands like the constant peacemaker he always was. "The order isn't 'shoot to kill.' You don't need to worry about a sniper or sneak attack."

"Right," Derek grumbled. "We are truly lucky."

Isaac continued seamlessly, ignoring the sarcasm. "Anyone coming for Allison will need time to get her to a second location, and she's already proven she won't go easily."

Derek narrowed his eyes. What Isaac described was better than a sniper, but only slightly. The fact that another attack on Allison was imminent, and apparently there was nothing they could do to stop it, was unacceptable. "We need to get her out of town without this guy realizing. How do we do that when we know he's watching?"

"I need things from my place, if we aren't going back," Allison said. "I understand why you want to take me somewhere else, but I can't go anywhere without Bonnie's basics. Formula, clothes, diapers, wipes. It'd be nice to have a proper place for her to sleep, as well. A thermometer, infant Tylenol, her stuffed bunny and favorite blanket."

Derek noticed Gwen nod empathetically. She'd been in Allison's place before, and understood better than anyone what she was going through. "Make a list," Gwen said. "Luke can pick it all up for you.

Maybe tell him where to look for everything." She turned to her fiancé. "Take a set of police duffels. Anyone watching will assume you're doing police business, setting up surveillance or something." She turned her attention back to Allison. "I'm sure you can borrow a portable crib from Blaze and Maisy."

Blaze drew the phone from his pocket. "I'll send her a text. Whatever you need."

Allison wiped her hands across her cheeks. "Thanks."

"That's what family's for," Gwen said, gaze flicking to Derek.

His chest tightened as his brothers grunted their agreement.

Was that what Allison and Bonnie were now? Family? And if so, what exactly did that make them to him? A strange ache began in his core, suggesting it was something to think about later. Right now, he needed a safe place for Allison and Bonnie. Somewhere they could disappear until the killers were caught.

"What about Clark?" Allison said suddenly. "He's at my place, and he's probably worried. We've been gone awhile, and he's been through a lot. What if he thinks we aren't coming back, either?"

Derek nearly laughed. She thought the dog had been through a lot? Hadn't she lost Mason, too? Then been shot at and nearly abducted twice? Was there anyone or anything Allison didn't worry about more than herself? "Our folks will take the dog," he assured her. "Dad loves that old hound, and Clark knows him well."

She sagged gently against him. "Good. He won't be afraid."

Gwen's eyes went round and her bottom lip seemed to push forward as her gaze swept from Allison to Derek. She was clearly already calculating ways to keep her.

Every woman in the family wanted more women in the family. It was pathological.

Derek shifted his weight, hating the next words he had to say. "Why don't one of you two detectives trade me hats and trucks."

Their combined shock was palpable.

Lucas palmed a set of keys and pushed them in Derek's direction. "Blaze drove the cruiser home last night and to work today. You can't drive that, so you get my truck. Be nice to it."

Derek accepted the offering, then reluctantly replaced it on his brother's palm with the key to his own truck. "Be. Careful."

Lucas's grin widened. "Absolutely."

He let his eyes drift shut for one long breath before accepting his fate—he'd be behind the wheel of a pickup slower than their mother's. "Meet us at my place in an hour?" Derek asked, lifting the cowboy hat from his head, as well. "Bring the dog. I'll have Mom and Dad meet you there to pick him up."

Lucas handed over his ball cap, then made a show of lowering the Stetson onto his head and adjusting the brim.

Gwen did a silent clap and beamed up at her beloved.

Of course, Allison had to be the one woman in town who didn't want a cowboy.

"Are we staying at your place?" Allison asked. "If Redmon was watching us at my house, then he surely has your license-plate number, and knows exactly who you are by now. He'll know where you live."

"That's not a problem," Derek said.

Blaze grunted, gaze fixed on his phone's screen. "We've got more thunderstorms headed this way tonight. If you're thinking of the family cabin, you'll want to head out tomorrow afternoon, when the rain stops and the road's had a chance to dry out. Even your truck wouldn't climb that trail in a mudslide," he said.

"Family cabin?" she asked, turning her face from Blaze to Derek.

"It's old and off the grid," Derek said. "There's a generator and running water. We'll be comfortable while these guys find Redmon, but Blaze's right. We'll need to hold tight tonight and leave once the sun's out. The road is overgrown, uphill, grass and dirt, no light. It's rough in the best of conditions. We'd be stuck in a heartbeat tonight, or worse, we'd slide right off the mountain."

Lucas spun Derek's key around one fingertip. "Maybe we should take this fancy truck out of town for the night," he told Gwen. "Someplace highly populated, where anyone following me would have a tough time pinning me down. Someplace in the opposite direction from Derek and Allison."

Gwen beamed. "I love it. We can take the bad guy on a wild-goose chase, then catch a show."

Allison stiffened. "I don't want to drag you into this any further than you already are," she told Gwen, a measure of horror and disbelief in her voice.

"I am already involved in this," Gwen said patiently. "It wasn't long ago that I was in trouble, too. And everyone who could help me when I needed it, did. I will absolutely do the same for you."

Lucas pulled her closer. "Where should we go?"

"Louisville," she said. "We'll stay downtown, where there's plenty of parking garages to help the truck disappear, and *Wicked* is playing at the State theater. I'll get tickets." She pulled out her phone out, and Lucas smiled.

Blaze clapped him on the back. "I'll follow you to Allison's place with my cruiser and the duffels. I'll wait half an hour after you leave before I go. Redmon should follow Derek's truck if he's watching the house. You can take Clark to Mom and Dad's on your way out of town. I'll take whatever Allison and Bonnie need to Derek's later, after I wrap up my shift and know I'm not being followed."

"We'll be back late tonight," Lucas vowed. "Meanwhile, I can put out some feelers and try to get a location on Redmon."

Allison took a seat at the conference table while the plan came together. She dragged a pen and pad of paper to her, and began to make her list. "How long will we be gone?" she asked. "I might need a few things, too."

"Just list everything," Derek said. "Better to have it and not need it, than to need it and not have it." Then he flashed his brothers a pointed look.

If they didn't make better progress on this investigation soon, he might be permanently relocating with Allison to a mountainside.

Chapter Eleven

The ride to Derek's house was shorter than Allison had expected. He lived on the same county road as she and Mason, but on the opposite side of downtown. When he'd stopped at the red light on Main Street, where she would've turned left and headed away from the quaint shopping area, Derek had turned right. He'd followed the curving two-lane road along the river for several miles, passing more livestock and farmland than homes or humans, then slowed at a gravel drive lined in pasture fencing.

A large Cape Cod–style home sat near the back of the property, where trees crowded the land. The wide slate-gray structure had a black door with matching trim around the broad windows and a steep black roof with three gables.

The acres of surrounding land were green and flat, punctuated by a stable, chicken coop and a small goat barn that resembled the house. A multitude of chickens dithered near the coop, and a pair of bearded pygmy goats grazed outside their little gray outbuilding.

Derek parked alongside the home, then hopped out, popped Bonnie's car seat away from the base and shouldered her diaper bag. "Everything okay?"

Allison nodded quickly, then climbed down and met him on the driver's side of his truck. "This is beautiful."

He smiled and it reached his eyes, lighting them and changing his features. The look erased years from his normally furrowed brow. "You want a tour?"

"Very much."

Derek carried the car seat and bag to his front porch, then left them there. He released Bonnie from the straps, laying her along his forearm and pulling her near, the way Allison had taught him.

Her heart stammered and swelled until she teared up. She smiled, instead of trusting her voice, then let him take the lead.

"I have twelve acres, the bulk of which is flat and workable. You can see most of it from here. The other four are wooded." He turned and extended an arm, indicating the trees behind the house. "The woods are mine along the river beyond my deck, then again on the other side. I have two horses," he said, continuing toward the stable. "Izzy and Cash. Izzy's been with me a long time. Cash came later."

Derek led her inside a beautifully crafted structure, much newer than his home. There were six stalls, three on each side. Izzy's and Cash's names had been burned into the wood of their respective doors. He stopped to stroke each giant nose and talk sweetly to them. "I bought Izzy from a friend's dad my senior year of high school. She lived with my folks while I was in the military, and I've been trying to make that up to her. I hadn't decided to enlist when I bought her, so I had a lot of guilt about leaving, not that my folks didn't spoil her. I got this guy about two years ago." He stroked the larger horse in the stall beside Izzy. "I thought she needed a companion. I foster horses sometimes, and she's always receptive to them, but Izzy deserved a permanent pal."

Allison smiled. "What kinds of horses do you foster?"

"Mostly sick or mistreated ones," he said, a look of profound sadness in his eyes. "Sometimes horses get that way because an owner is mean and doesn't deserve to have them. Other times, an owner gets older and can't care for the animals properly anymore, either physically or financially. When they have too much pride to accept a handout, the health of the animal can go downhill quickly. Vets around here know they can bring those horses to me, and I'll keep them while they mend. I just dropped a pair off at their forever home the morning I met you."

"That was why you had the trailer," she said.

"Yeah. I'd planned to stop at Mason's and tell him about it before heading home. Now, it's just me and these two again." He gave each horse another dose of love before heading back the way they'd come. "I'll let them out once I get you settled."

Allison squinted against the sunlight as they moved toward the house. "You have so many chickens," she said, smiling at the crew of chubby birds headed their way.

He looked at them and laughed. "Yes. That's a bad habit of mine. I buy one or two from the 4-H kids at the county fair every year, and they've started to add up. I plan to bring Mason's hens down here to live with these guys."

She watched as he scattered feed over the ground with one hand, cradling Bonnie with the other, as if it was the most natural thing in the world.

Bonnie alternated between squinting against the sun and marveling at the sights. She'd especially seemed interested in the horses.

Derek put away the feed, then dusted his free hand against his jeans. His smile picked up as he looked toward the goats. "That's Jack and Jill," he said, leading her to a pair of pygmies grazing inside a fence. "I'll visit with them when I come out to care for Izzy and Cash."

Allison wanted to meet the goats, too, but knew she and Bonnie would only slow him down, so she didn't mention it. "Thank you for letting us stay tonight," she said instead. "We won't be any trouble."

He rolled his eyes, sliding easily back into brooding-PI mode. He lifted the car seat and diaper bag when they reached the porch.

"Let me help you," she said, tugging the bag and seat from his hand. "You can't carry everything. You're not a pack mule."

He snorted a laugh as he turned the knob and

stepped inside with Bonnie. "Welcome to your temporary home."

Allison smiled. It was nice that he hadn't called it his home, though it was. Instead, he'd made an effort to make her feel less like a guest from her first step inside. "Thanks." She turned in a semicircle, taking in the open floor plan.

A small foyer opened into a large central living area with a fireplace, a television and seating. Cathedral ceilings soared overhead, the stone from a beautiful fireplace rising all the way to the top. Several tall swivel chairs lined an island, separating the living space from the kitchen. And a set of narrow stairs led to a loft overlooking the entire space.

"This is incredible," she said, gaze roaming over the decor before settling on a set of windows that showcased a patio and pergola out back.

"I renovated it with my dad and brothers," he said. "It's still a bit of a work in progress."

Unlike her home, which was decorated with an abundance of color, everything at Derek's place seemed to be black or gray. The furniture was large, overstuffed and broken-in. The kitchen had newer stainless-steel appliances, but aged, unpainted cabinets.

"Living room, kitchen, patio," he said, pointing into each space from where he stood. "Bathroom, bedrooms, laundry." He extended a hand to the hallway beyond the kitchen, then motioned for her to follow. "I'll show you where to put your things."

They passed three open doors, slowly, so she

could peek inside each one. The guest bath was done in all white. White tiles. White towels. White countertops and fixtures. Even a white rug centered the white tiled floor. The guest bedroom was much the same, except with a pale gray comforter and multicolored braided rug. Even the laundry room was in perfect order. White on white, like the other rooms, save for the detergent bottles and a stack of folded jeans.

He hesitated outside the only partially closed door, then pushed it open and moved inside. "You and Bonnie can set up in here. It's the master bedroom, so you won't have to go into the hallway to use the bathroom or get ready for your day. I'll strip the bed and change the sheets when I come in from tending to the animals. Meanwhile, you should make yourselves at home. I keep the kitchen fully stocked. If you get hungry or want coffee, consider it yours. And the view out back is worth seeing."

Allison tried not to stare at the large bed against the wall, its pale gray sheets pulled back against a matching duvet that looked soft as butter. The pillows were askew, the blankets mussed. He'd woken on a day like any other yesterday, she realized, probably expecting to be back that night. Instead, she'd nearly run him off the road, and he hadn't been home since. "We can take the guest room," she said, certain his pillowcases would smell like him, and already curious about the type of body wash she'd find in his shower.

He gave the diaper bag and car seat a pointed look,

then tipped his head to the bed. "Leave those here. I'll take the guest room."

She released the items, reluctantly, appreciation welling in her chest once more.

Derek watched her, his gaze cautious and guarded, as if there was something else he wanted to say.

Bonnie twitched, and his gaze dropped to the infant in his arms. She'd fallen asleep against his chest, her tiny mouth moving in sweet baby circles. Dreaming of her next meal, no doubt.

Allison pressed a hand against the growing ache behind her ribs. The place where her pooling emotions were fast reaching capacity. She inhaled a shaky breath and her lips parted.

Heat flamed in Derek's eyes, and she wondered again if he felt it, too, this mind-boggling, bone-melting chemistry that simmered between them all the time, then seemed to blaze to life anytime they were alone.

As if in answer, Derek's attention lowered to her mouth.

THE SOUND OF tires on gravel startled Derek from the moment of perfect tension. He followed Allison's gaze as it jerked toward the bedroom window.

A new white Ford trundled down his driveway, kicking up clouds of dust among the gravel. "Is it too soon to meet my parents?" he asked, allowing a smile to curl around the words.

She snickered. "I'm not sure there's a protocol for what we've got going on. So why not?"

Derek led the way back to the front door, Bonnie snoring softly in his arms. "If they're here, it's safe to say my brother's already delivered Clark to their place." And his parents were anxious to get a look at Allison and her baby.

Allison moved into the space behind him at the door. "Earlier, you said you weren't afraid the killer would trace the truck to your house instead of following it? Why? And how can you be so sure?"

"Truck's registered to the PI firm, and I bought this place under an LLC for rehabilitating horses. I knew better than to make a local PI's home address easy to find."

"Oh," she said, seeming relieved. "Smart."

"I try."

His folks climbed down from the truck with wide eyes and eager expressions. They were definitely here to see the baby.

He barely got the front door open before his mom pulled the sleeping infant from his arms.

"Oh, my heavens she's perfect!" she squealed, turning the infant to her chest and snuggling her close.

"Mom, that is Bonnie, Allison's baby," he said, motioning his parents inside. "This is Allison Hill."

Allison had moved against the wall, outside of the middle-aged, two-human stampede zone that was his parents, while sticking close enough to save her baby if needed. "Hi," she said, gaze darting from Bonnie to the stranger now holding her.

Derek's mother patted his chest on her way to wrap Allison in a hug. "I'm Rosa," she said. "You can call me Mom, everyone does. This is Hank. Say hi, Hank."

"Hello." His dad tipped his hat, nearly drooling for his turn to hold the baby.

"Thanks for dog-sitting," Derek said. "We appreciate that."

"We?" his mom asked, releasing Allison and turning curious eyes on Derek.

"Allison and…me," he said, realizing then that saying "we" really hadn't made sense. Clark was Mason's dog, not his or Allison's. They certainly didn't own him jointly, and they weren't a couple.

Did he want to be? Did she? Did it matter?

His mom smiled politely, either intrigued or bored by his lack of answer. "Well, *we*," she said, casting a look at his father, "heard you needed baby things, so we packed up all our grandparent materials and brought them over so your brothers won't need to haul all of Allison's things down from her place. If the house is being watched, that would look all kinds of suspicious. You'll need to reassemble the crib, but the swing, high chair and general items only need a destination. Where should we put them?"

"Anywhere," Allison said, her expression bursting with gratitude.

"And the crib?" his mom asked.

"My room," Derek said, then lifted a hand in awkward clarification. "The ladies are staying in the master tonight, so they'll have an attached bath. I'm in the guest room."

And based on the level of discomfort this conversation was causing him, he was approximately fifteen years old again.

His mom returned her attention to Allison. "How are you holding up?" she asked. "Why don't I fix us something to drink while Derek helps Hank bring in the baby things?"

Derek turned and clapped his dad on the back, thankful for the exit. "We won't be long," he warned. "Only say nice things, or I might hear you."

His dad made a disappointed, throaty noise. "When we get done, it's my turn to hold the baby."

"Absolutely," Derek said, jogging down the steps toward his father's truck, eager to finish the chore and return to Allison.

ALLISON SETTLED BONNIE into the crib Derek's parents had so graciously provided, then carried the baby monitor's speaker with her as she crept from the room.

Derek was on the back deck, cleaning up their meal. He'd grilled fish for an early dinner, then sent the leftovers with his parents.

Now, with an early evening sun sinking toward the horizon, Allison suppressed the urge to panic. There was a killer on the loose. With explicit instructions to bring her to his boss. A boss who was apparently someone even a killer feared.

Derek noticed her approach through the sliding doors and smiled. Wind lifted his soft brown hair, flying free from the confines of his usual cowboy hat, which was on its way to Louisville. Along with his truck, brother, Gwen and hopefully the nut who was hunting Allison.

She stepped onto the deck, wrapping her arms around her middle. "I love this weather," she confessed, tipping her face to the sky. "I know I'm not supposed to, but I do. Always have."

Derek turned to stand at her side. "Spring storms?"

"All storms. I've never once had the sense to come out of the rain. Unless there's lightning," she said, peeking at him from the corner of her eye. "In those cases, I'm not happy about it." She dropped her hands to her side, then turned to smile at Derek, hoping to ease some of the ever-present tension between them, but something in his eyes removed the chill from her skin.

"You were great with my parents," he said, his voice a little rough and unsure. "They can be a lot to take, but you did really well. They aren't big on boundaries."

"I liked your parents," she said easily, and meant it. "I can appreciate that they're unguarded. It made me feel like they were being themselves, not putting on a show for my sake. And if that's true, then maybe they aren't saying mean things about me all the way home." She frowned at the thought. She'd known plenty of people like that over the years. "Your folks made up for any lack of boundaries with an abundance of love and affection."

Derek's eyebrows tented briefly in surprise before sinking together once more. "I've known my share of folks like the ones you described. I guess it's easier to be on guard than to be kicked when you're not looking."

Allison turned to stare. It was hard to imagine someone like Derek Winchester being kicked around by anyone. Or caring if someone tried. He seemed more like the type everyone immediately respected and adored. "I'm sorry you've been through that," she said. "Some people can be terrible."

"Yeah," he agreed, a familiar cocky smile teasing his lips. "But others are pretty great."

He was certainly right about that. She bit her bottom lip, drawing his attention there, and the electricity crackled between them. She imagined the skies opening and the rain pouring. Then, Derek kissing her senseless in the storm.

"I should bring the horses in," he said. "Walk with me?"

She followed him through his evening routine, helping when she could, and petting every creature who'd tolerate it, from horse to chicken to barn cat. She couldn't help wondering what it would be like to live someplace surrounded with so many animals and so much love.

"What?" Derek asked, steering her back toward the house when the work was done.

"Nothing." She dusted her palms together, unable to stop the smile. "It's nice here. That's all."

"You like it?"

"Who wouldn't?" she asked. "It's great. Clark will be really happy here. So will Mason's hens. They're lucky, and you're very kind to take them on when you're already busy running a business and saving the world one damsel at a time."

Derek laughed. "Are you supposed to be the damsel in that statement?"

She shrugged. "I'm definitely in distress, and you're currently protecting me from harm."

"When I'm not putting you in it," he said, voice dropping to an apologetic groan.

"You've never put me in danger," she said, slowing her pace to fix him with a pointed stare.

"Maybe not intentionally, but I leave, then trouble comes," he said. "I was naive and careless the first time. It was downright stupid the second. Smart people learn from their mistakes, they don't repeat them."

"Hey." She stopped short, and grabbed his wrist as he tried to pass. "Neither of those things were your fault."

He squinted, his gaze moving to the place where her fingers gripped his skin. "I don't want to argue."

"Good, because I'm right," she said, forcing her hand to release him. "Can we walk on your dock before we go inside?" The river always grew agitated before a storm, and it was her favorite part. As if the water somehow sensed what was coming and grew excited, along with her.

Derek led her onto the dock, then slowed to let her pass.

She savored the sounds of their footsteps across the weathered and sun-bleached boards. Puffy white clouds raced through an amber-and-apricot sky as the sun sank lower behind the trees.

The river was wider at this point than she'd expected, and the ripples glimmered for what seemed like miles. She'd need a boat to cross the water here, unlike behind her property, where anyone could easily swim the expanse in a few minutes.

"Do you ever go boating?" he asked.

"I have," she said. "But I get seasick pretty easily on a boat. I love swimming. Fishing. Tubing. Kayaking. All of that. But boats and I don't always get along." She gave the enchanting scene around her another look. "You're really lucky to have such great access here."

"I have kayaks and a canoe, if you're ever interested." He smiled, then pulled his eyes away. "My brothers and I grew up on the water. Dad's a river nut and a history buff. Get him started on the history of this river, and he'll be talking all day. We used to make these crazy long-haul canoe trips that took days. We'd pull off and camp on the shores, then get up at first light and go again. For days. We'd pack all our food and supplies, plus the four of us, sometimes five, in two canoes. Mom would pick us up at the end and bring us home. The scenery's breathtaking in some places with insanely high bluffs that made me feel like I was in an Indiana Jones movie."

"Sounds like fun," she said. "It's kind of crazy to think that this water runs around six states, including ours, before meeting the Mississippi."

Derek smiled. "You know your river trivia. Dad would be proud."

She laughed. Then something curious wiggled into mind. "This river runs from Pennsylvania to the Gulf of Mexico," she said, a strange idea forming.

Derek pulled his phone from his pocket, seeming to have a similar thought.

"The water's a major mode of transport for a lot of things," she said. Her stomach pitted as the words fell from her tongue. "Including women."

Chapter Twelve

Derek led Allison back inside and locked up carefully behind them. It was unnerving to think Mason's killers could be using the river to move abducted women. Even scarier to know it wouldn't be hard with the right connections and a little planning. Most boats passed easily on the water, moving from port to port and state to state with little trouble.

Allison set the baby monitor on the kitchen island. A peaceful night-vision image of Bonnie centered the screen. "Did you text Blaze?"

Derek nodded, hoping their theory was wrong. The number of women living in river towns, who could become prey in a single day, was terrifying. He knew and cared about enough people in his town alone for the concept to hit like a punch to the chest. "Yeah, he's coming by after his shift." He released a restless sigh as he headed around the island and into the kitchen. Regardless of whether this theory was right or wrong, these criminals had to be stopped, and he doubted he'd sleep again until they were all behind bars. "How do you feel about coffee?"

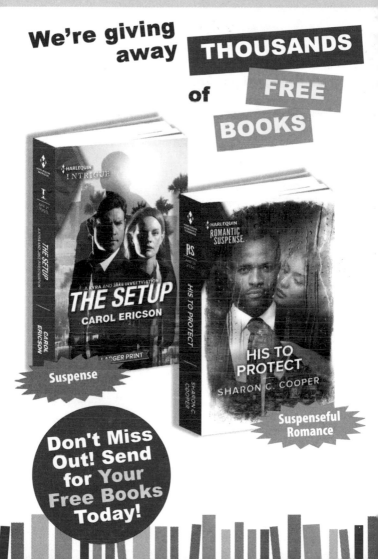

Get up to 4 FREE FABULOUS BOOKS You Love!

To thank you for being a loyal reader we'd like to send you up to 4 FREE BOOKS, absolutely free.

Just write "YES" on the Loyal Reader Voucher and we'll send you up to 4 Free Books and Free Mystery Gifts, altogether worth over $20, as a way of saying thank you for being a loyal reader.

Try **Harlequin® Romantic Suspense** books featuring heart-racing page-turners with unexpected plot twists and irresistible chemistry that will keep you guessing to the very end.

Try **Harlequin Intrigue® Larger-Print** books featuring action-packed stories that will keep you on the edge of your seat. Solve the crime and deliver justice at all costs.

Or **TRY BOTH!**

We are so glad you love the books as much as we do and can't wait to send you great new books.

So don't miss out, return your Loyal Reader Voucher Today!

Pam Powers

LOYAL READER
FREE BOOKS VOUCHER

YES! I Love Reading, please send me up to 4 FREE BOOKS and Free Mystery Gifts from the series I select.

Just write in "YES" on the dotted line below then return this card today and we'll send your free books & gifts asap!

➡ _____ YES _____ ⬅

Which do you prefer?

| ☐ **Harlequin® Romantic Suspense** 240/340 HDL GRHP | ☐ **Harlequin Intrigue® Larger-Print** 199/399 HDL GRHP | ☐ **BOTH** 240/340 & 199/399 HDL GRHZ |

FIRST NAME _____ LAST NAME _____

ADDRESS _____

APT.# _____ CITY _____

STATE/PROV. _____ ZIP/POSTAL CODE _____

EMAIL ☐ Please check this box if you would like to receive newsletters and promotional emails from Harlequin Enterprises ULC and its affiliates. You can unsubscribe anytime.

HI/HRS-520-LR21

"Yes, please," she said. "I don't expect to sleep tonight. Might as well at least be alert."

Derek tried not to imagine how he would pass the night with Allison, awake, while keeping his hands to himself. But he was nothing if not self-controlled. Maybe enough coffee would also keep him on his feet and moving. "Coming right up."

He set the pot to brew, then checked the time. "Will Bonnie be up again soon?" The presence of her baby would also serve as a great reminder that this wasn't some kind of complicated date they were on. Allison was a single mom in need of his services. *His protection services*. Nothing more.

"She'll wake for a bottle around eleven tonight, then sleep until around six tomorrow morning." Allison checked her watch. "We should have a few hours of quiet time until then."

It was barely seven.

Derek leaned against the kitchen countertop, hoping Blaze would drop by sooner rather than later.

Her fair eyebrows furrowed as she watched him. "Do you think the notes on the scrap of paper I found at Mason's could be some kind of coordinates?"

Derek shook his head. "No, but I took a photo of the paper. We can take a look at it while we wait for Blaze if you want."

She smiled. "Maybe we'll have another idea to hit him with when he arrives."

"We might as well just solve this thing for him and be done with it."

"Exactly." Allison laughed. "I'm not sure why

we're just sitting around like this. We should be working." She scanned the countertops on either side of him. "Do you have a pad of paper and pen? We can copy the notations from the photo to make them easier to work with."

"In the loft," he said, trading the slowly filling pot for a big blue mug. "I'll run up in a minute." The mug filled, and he swapped it for a second empty one.

"I can grab the notebook," she said, already moving toward the stairs. "It's no problem, if you don't mind. Is it on your desk?"

"Yeah." He replaced the pot and abandoned the freshly filled mugs, then hurried to her side. "I'll come with you. My desk is a mess."

His chest pinched as he followed her upward, wishing he had a reason to keep her downstairs.

She smiled as she reached the top step. "So, this is where you live?"

"When I'm home and have to be indoors," he said.

The loft was a cluttered mess compared to the rest of the house, because she was right. This was where he spent his time. After work and animal care, general chores and property maintenance. The filing cabinets and bookcases were weighted down with tomes and research, an arsenal of PI tools and a slew of memorabilia from his life on horseback.

"Wow." She tapped one finger against the desk, where piles of papers and folders stood in uneven stacks around a calendar embarrassingly dusted in crumbs from meals eaten as he worked. "You weren't kidding about being part of the rodeo."

He bit his tongue as he followed her gaze to the shelf of photos, ribbons and memories.

"Look at you." She smiled at a cluster of childhood photos from local parades, county fairs and FFA meetings. "Future Farmers of America, huh?"

He laughed, shoving his hands into his front pockets. "Yep." He'd loved all things cowboy the way some kids loved superheroes. And his folks had indulged him, providing lessons on roping, riding and all things wrangler-related.

Allison lifted a set of medals and ribbons thick with dust. "'Mutton busting champion,'" she read. "Two years in a row."

"Kindergarten and first grade," he said, both tense and a little proud. He'd worked hard to learn to ride those sheep, and winning twice in a county full of young kids like himself was no easy task.

"What happened here?" she asked, crossing her arms and flicking her gaze toward a framed newspaper article and photo of him being thrown from the toughest bull he'd ever known. A local reporter caught the shot, while he was airborne, a moment before his life flashed before his eyes, and he remembered what mattered. The concern in Allison's eyes made him want to tell her the truth in a way he rarely ever did.

"I was thrown, and nearly killed," he said, putting it as bluntly and simply as possible. "That was my last ride." He scanned her face, searching for a sign he'd said too much, but there was only sincere interest in her big blue eyes.

"What'd you do?" she asked.

"Once I healed, I followed the rest of my family's footsteps to the police academy." Derek plucked a pen from his desk and set it atop a spiral notebook. "I whipped through the courses and the civil-service exam without any trouble. Then I was paired up with an older cop who had no interest in training a rookie. A few weeks into our uncomfortable partnership, we were supposed to make a big drug bust. He'd been putting the case together for years. I guess he didn't want to share the glory, because he took off without me, and it took me a while to realize what was happening. Once I figured out where he went, I followed, but by the time I got there, the place was empty, completely cleared out. And my partner had been shot four times. I stayed with him, called an ambulance, then his wife. I held the phone while he said goodbye." Derek worked his jaw to keep the freight train of emotions at bay. That night had been more than two years ago, but it still felt like yesterday. And he still shrank back when he saw the officer's wife or kids in town. Because they knew. Derek had lost track of his partner. He wasn't where he needed to be that night. And their family lost a husband and father because of it.

He braced himself for Allison's follow-up questions. Her pity, or her repulsion.

"Derek," she whispered, sincere concern coloring her cheeks as she stepped cautiously forward and pulled him into a gentle hug. "I'm sorry you went through that, and I'm really glad you told me.

I think it means you trust me, and I like that. Also," she added after a long beat, "I'm thankful you became a PI. Bonnie and I wouldn't have survived this long without you."

His arms closed over her as he processed her words. "I'm not sure that's true, but I'm willing to take the compliment," he said. "And I do trust you."

It was frightening how much.

"Since we're being honest," she said, turning her face upward, and pinning him with an apologetic smile, "I judged you unfairly before, because of what happened with my ex. But you're nothing like him. You're a far better man, brother, son and friend. I was wrong to judge you before I knew you."

Derek's fingers curved against her sides, urging her impossibly closer. It would be so easy to turn the gentle embrace into something more. To lower his lips to hers and take her mouth in a kiss that would surely leave them both seeing stars.

"Derek?" she whispered, palms sliding up his chest to his shoulders, her gaze drifting to his lips, as if she'd been thinking the same thing.

His head tipped forward, his mouth drawn to hers by something much stronger than his waning control.

The doorbell rang, and she jumped back, yanking her hands away and blushing furiously.

Derek groaned as he pulled his phone from his pocket to check the camera at his door. "My brother and his perfect timing," he said, lifting a wry smile to meet her shy gaze.

"I am so sorry," she whispered. "I'm never like this. I don't know what's gotten into me."

He shook his head, grabbed the pen and pad, then took her hand and led her back down the steps to the front door, nowhere near ready to let her go. "How about we agree to talk about it after our company leaves?" he asked, enjoying the *we* and *our* in that sentence more than he ever dreamed he could.

Chapter Thirteen

Derek poured three fresh mugs of coffee, after dumping the two that had gone cold. Then he joined Blaze and Allison at the kitchen island, offering a mug to each.

Blaze unloaded the contents of a messenger bag onto the counter. A laptop and power cord first, then several photographs, along with copies of paperwork Derek recognized as coming from the local crime lab.

Lightning flashed and thunder boomed outside the sliding doors, as ominous and foreboding as a scene in any crime thriller, and for the first time in his life, Derek wished that was where they were. Because in fictional worlds, the bad guys went to jail, and the heroes saved the day. Derek hadn't felt much like a hero since the moment he'd realized Mason had been murdered in his home, and Derek hadn't had a clue. The two attempted abductions on Allison since then had only made his feelings of ineptitude more profound. Telling her about his time on the police force had driven it all home. She knew now that a man died on his watch. Whether his partner took off on his own or not, he was Derek's partner. His to protect. And he'd failed.

He couldn't fail again.

Thunder boomed, rattling the windows and causing Bonnie to stir in her sleep. Her tiny protests vibrated through the monitor Allison never let out of her reach.

The storm that had been blowing in all evening had finally arrived, and their little town was in for a long, rough night.

Allison wrapped her hands around the steaming mug, then turned her eyes to Blaze. "How's it going with the truck swap?" she asked. "Have Lucas and Gwen made it to Louisville? Do they know if they were followed?"

Derek leaned a hip against the counter, anxious to hear his brother's response.

Had their plan worked? Did Lucas draw the killer away? Or was Allison's assailant somehow lurking outside Derek's home, even now? Maybe even using the storm for cover.

"They arrived about an hour ago," Blaze said. "They parked the truck in an underground parking deck, then went to dinner before the show. They're going to drive home tonight, so Lucas can help me follow up on your river theory. As an SVU detective, he has some connections who might know something about it, especially if we're looking at possible sex trafficking."

Allison's fair skin paled further. "So, we might be right?"

"It's definitely possible," Blaze said. "The handful of recently missing women seems to support the theory."

She set down the mug with a rattle, then reached for the printouts in front of her. "We need to save these girls."

Blaze shot Derek a curious look.

Derek shrugged in return. Allison looked fragile, but she just kept surprising him.

She turned the photographs of trace evidence to face her. Five strands of hair pulled from Mason's shirt. "What else do you know?" she asked Blaze, quietly, lifting wide blue eyes to his.

He sipped his coffee, lowering his eyes and scanning the papers before them. "The lab confirmed the hairs are from four different blond women. The blood matches the DNA from one of those. The fifth hair was jet-black. Possibly dyed." He sifted through the pile of papers and printouts, then turned a set of missing-person flyers toward her, as well. "The lab's working with the families of these women, to match the hairs with DNA from their homes. Once we can confirm the identities, we can saturate local news and media outlets with the images. If everyone in the state is looking for these ladies, it could help us get a bead on their current location."

"If their captors let them see the light of day," Allison said, unwittingly voicing Derek's thoughts with her own.

He looked through the photos and papers, examining each carefully. There were four more missing-person flyers beneath the two of special interest. "All these women vanished in the past month?" He ran a finger over the personal details, seeking a connection between the six. "Are they all from river towns?"

"No," Blaze said, lifting a finger to indicate there was something more. "Which is probably why we didn't pick up on the connection to the river earlier. They weren't all from towns like ours, but they all went missing from one." He pulled a pair of photos away from the rest. "These women live nearly an hour from the nearest river access, but they were each visiting a town with a port when they went missing."

Allison's lips pressed into a thin white line, and she covered them with slender fingers. "They're so young."

"Fourteen and sixteen. Of these six, the oldest woman is twenty-five," Blaze said. "But even she could pass for a high-schooler." He cast a wary look at Derek before swinging his attention back to Allison. "It's been bugging me more and more how much you fit into the general profile here." His gaze flickered to the photos.

Derek's muscles locked. The thought of Allison as a victim of sex trafficking made him want to strike. Heat pooled in his core, rising through his chest and neck, then spilling over his face. He reviewed the missing-person flyers again, examining each woman and her details. Blaze was right about Allison fitting the mold. She was twenty-three, but looked much younger. She was thin and well-groomed, with long hair, clear skin and blue eyes.

He swore.

Allison shot him a curious look, then pulled the flyers closer to her, flipping through them and slowly turning green, presumably with nausea. Derek certainly wanted to be sick just imagining such a horrific possibility. "I could've been another face on one of these flyers."

Derek growled, the low, unintentional sound vibrating in his throat. His hands curled into fists at his sides, and a muscle flexed in his jaw.

"No," she said, eyes going wide before filling with infinite sadness. "I wouldn't be on a flyer, because no one would've known I was gone." She swallowed, then continued her heartbreaking thought. "If these guys had taken me and Bonnie that first day, neither of us would've survived. Because no one would've looked for us. I'm still on maternity leave, and I'm not particularly close with anyone at work. We don't have family or friends in the area who'd have suspected we were in danger or come looking for us." Allison sucked in a shuddering breath and wiped tears from her cheeks with frantic, jerky motions. "Sorry. I just can't…"

Derek handed her a tissue. "Don't worry about it. This is a lot, and for what it's worth, you have family now. You have friends. And we'll always know if you need help. We'll know, and we'll be there."

Blaze nodded. "Agreed. And if you feel up to it, it would be really helpful if you can take another look through the criminal database. See if another mug shot stands out. Identifying the other man you saw outside Mason's home and yours could be exactly what we need to break this case. The second man could be the boss. Knowing that would be incredibly helpful in finding these women. We're already digging into known accomplices, family, friends and places of previous arrests for Redmon. Naming the second guy opens a new world of connections and potential informants."

Derek eyed the laptop Blaze had yet to power up. "Can you log in from here? Because we need to leave tomorrow when the rain stops, and I'd rather not make another trip to the station."

Blaze tapped a finger to his temple, then opened the laptop.

Allison stared at the photos of the missing women, nodding her silent agreement to give the database another look. "Why do you think the killers are still here?" she asked. "What are they waiting for? I know Redmon says someone wants me, but I wasn't one of their targets. I was a fluke who complicated things for them. Maybe the boss wants to punish me for that, but is it really worth the risk of staying in a place where local law enforcement is actively looking for them? Why not take off? They could be all the way to New Orleans by now."

Derek rubbed the back of his neck. She had a very good question.

Why weren't the criminals more worried about being caught? Why stick around?

"I don't know," Blaze said finally. "But I'm guessing whatever the reason, it isn't good."

"What about the paper Allison found near the chicken coop?" Derek asked. "Any chance that's a lead to where they're going next, or where we can find them?"

"Maybe." Blaze sifted through the papers again. He pulled out an enlarged image of the paper Allison had been wise enough to pocket when she spotted it in the mud. "We're working on it, but right now, your guess is as good as mine. I'm thinking the notations might be abbreviations for dates, times or zip codes. Something broken down but not heavily coded. I have no idea what, or if this paper even belonged to them. We could be wasting precious time decoding a litterbug's cheat sheet for midterms."

Allison opened the notebook Derek had retrieved from his office and flipped to a blank page, then poised the pen above it. "I'll play with the notations for a while if you don't mind."

"Sure," Blaze said. "I'll log in to the criminal database, then leave it up for you, when you're ready."

ALLISON PUSHED ASIDE the notepad once the laptop was ready. Blaze was right. They didn't know for certain that the paper was a real clue. They did, however, know the criminal database was a solid place to look for people like the men who'd killed Mason and broke into her home. The mug shots had to take priority.

An unnerving sense of déjà vu swept through her

as she scrolled, and she had to suppress the shiver that came with it. The last time she'd looked through the database, a lunatic had grabbed her an hour later.

Thunder rolled outside, and she jumped in response.

The Winchesters were polite enough not to mention it, though she was certain they'd both noticed. Very little seemed to get past either of them as far as she could see.

Allison examined the images on screen, no longer sure she'd recognize the second guy if she saw him. Her mind was tired and full of awful things. Her memory of the second man was blurry and faded. It would be a near miracle if she could pick him out in a lineup of two people, let alone a database of thousands.

"How are things going on your end?" Blaze asked.

Allison raised her eyes to the brothers.

Blaze's attention was fixed on Derek, whose gaze was hard and frame was rigid.

"As good as expected," Derek said, forcing a tight smile. "Dad said things are in order at the cabin. He and Mom were there last weekend. We should have everything we need, minus some groceries we can pick up on the way."

"How are you feeling about it?" Blaze asked. "You seem tense."

Derek stretched his neck, tipping his head over one shoulder, then the other. He glanced at Allison, who quickly looked away. "I am. I've never been on a trip like this with a baby, and one tiny person changes things."

Allison frowned at him, the laptop, and all pretense of not listening, forgotten. "Bonnie won't be any trouble," she said defensively. "I'll take care of whatever she needs."

"I know." Derek's expression turned grim, but apologetic. "But babies cry. They can't be reasoned with, and they don't understand what's at stake. If the perimeter I set is breached, or if you have to hide, it's not as if you can tell her to be quiet and still so you won't be found."

Allison opened her mouth to argue, but couldn't. Everything he'd said was true, and he hadn't been angry or cruel about it.

"She also can't run," Derek continued. "She can't follow simple commands to save her life or yours, and all those things make her a liability. I'm not saying any of this to be negative. I'm just running through worst-case scenarios in my head, troubleshooting, planning, trying to figure out what we do if this or that comes to pass. It's all trickier with a baby."

Allison fought to swallow the lump in her throat. "I can't leave her."

"I know."

Blaze watched as they spoke, eyes narrowing. "Bottom line," he said, "is that you're all going to be just fine. Derek will set a strong and defensible perimeter at the cabin. Lucas, my team and I will make sure no one knows you're there. And we'll be turning over every rock in the county searching for Redmon or someone who knows him. The expression 'thick as thieves' only holds true until you find one thief's bargaining chip. Someone who knows him will gladly give him up for the right price. A reduced sentence for someone they love, who's serving time, or leniency on whatever charges we can bring up. Maybe even cash. But they all have a price."

Derek rounded the island to Blaze's side. "You're right. We've got this." He gave his brother a quick hug and fist bump. "Thanks, for the reminder."

Their voices lowered, and their words drifted into acronyms and unfamiliar terminology, until the shop talk went completely over her head.

Allison turned her attention back to the laptop, her thoughts racing and her mind more desperate than ever to identify the second man she'd seen at Mason's home and hers. She had to do whatever she could to help the detectives locate and arrest the men planning to abduct her. More than that, they needed to save the missing women before they were gone for good. She easily imagined herself in their position. Frightened, alone and possibly sold into sex trafficking.

The small muddy footprints outside Mason's house came to mind, and Allison felt the emotions building once more. One woman in the clutches of those awful, evil men hadn't given up. And neither could she.

That woman had run. She'd sought the help of a stranger. Barefoot in the cold. And alone.

That woman had to be saved. If it wasn't already too late.

Allison scrolled more slowly through the mug shots, willing one of them to be familiar.

Blaze's phone rang, and the brothers sprang apart

from their tiny two-man huddle. "Winchester," Blaze answered, listening carefully. His sharp gray-blue eyes latched on Derek as he disconnected the short, but clearly disturbing, call.

"What?" Allison asked, abandoning the laptop and drifting closer to the protectors before her. "Did something happen?"

Blaze's livid expression sent a wave of chills down her spine. "Yeah. Another teen just went missing."

Chapter Fourteen

Allison woke to Bonnie's happy coos. She yawned and stretched beneath the impossibly soft sheets, smiling at her infant, who was contentedly wiggling in the crib beside Allison's bed.

Derek had changed the sheets for her, but he'd forgotten the pillowcase, and it smelled exactly like his warm hugs. The fresh, earthy scent of the outdoors, interlaced with a cologne-and-body-wash combination she was beginning to associate with him alone.

She shed the toasty, comfy blankets and swung her feet onto the floor, eager to get her arms around her precious baby. "Good morning, sweet girl," she whispered, pulling Bonnie from the crib. "You had a big night's sleep for such a little lady." According to the clock on the nightstand, Bonnie had slept eight consecutive hours. A personal record. Allison, on the other hand, had struggled to put more than a few minutes of rest together at a time. Her mind had been busy reviewing her fears and worries. Replaying the awful things she'd seen and experienced these past few days, along with a slew of horrific possibilities her imagination had conjured for the days ahead.

The raging storm outside hadn't helped. Whistling winds. Booming thunder. And the slosh of rain against the windows had only served to punctuate her unease until late in the night.

Now, with sunlight streaming through the glass, and her baby snuggled in her arms, Allison was hit with a fresh rush of adrenaline and purpose. She rushed through the morning routine, preparing herself and Bonnie to greet their host and ask for a favor.

Allison dressed in faded jeans and a long-sleeved blue T-shirt, then tugged fuzzy white socks over her feet. Bonnie wore a similar outfit, though her top was polka-dotted with cartoon ladybugs and her pants pockets were outlined in lace. A few strokes of Allison's hairbrush, toothbrush and mascara wand later, and the Hill ladies were ready to go. She'd done her best to cover the darkening bruise on her forehead with a little concealer, but makeup application had never been her strongest skill. In the end, her thin fringe of bangs was the better camouflage.

She opened the bedroom door and nearly groaned in anticipation. Based on both the sweet scent of syrup and rich aroma of pancakes hanging in the air, Derek was already up and making breakfast.

Soft country music drifted from the kitchen as she and Bonnie drew near. Derek sang along with the familiar lyrics as he transferred pancakes from a griddle to a nearby platter. "Hey," he said, smiling at the sight of them. "I hope you like pancakes."

"I love pancakes." She stopped at the counter to assemble Bonnie's bottle, trying not to stare at her handsome protector.

He was so at home in his kitchen, barefoot and whipping up a meal to share with her. He was at ease with the animals and with his family. Doing his job or just hanging out. Derek was comfortable in his skin. Confident and self-assured in ways she aspired to be. And her admiration of him grew a little more with each passing experience at his side.

"Get any sleep?" he asked, casting a warm smile her way.

"Not really." She gave the bottle a hearty shake as she spoke. "I kept thinking of those women being torn from their lives. The shock and pain and helplessness. I can't imagine how frightened they must be now, especially those who've been gone awhile, who probably don't think they'll ever make it home again. And those poor teenagers." She tipped the bottle to Bonnie's mouth, thankful her daughter was here in her arms, and guilty for the selfish thought when so many mothers would never hold their babies again.

Derek poured two mugs of coffee from the pot, then carried them to the table of his eat-in kitchen, already set for two. A high chair was positioned on one side.

"Thanks," she said, eagerly following him and her future energy source. "Any chance Blaze has more information on the girl who went missing last night?"

"Not yet, but it's early." Derek doubled back to the kitchen counter, then returned with the tray of pancakes and a bottle of syrup.

Allison reclined the high chair's seat to accommodate her princess, then secured her with the straps. "How long have you been up?" she asked Derek.

A small smile touched his lips as he settled onto a chair. His eyes flicked quickly to the front door, then the back. "Awhile."

Allison followed his gaze to stacks of boxes, bags and luggage arranged in the foyer. "You've already packed for the cabin? You really have been busy."

He shrugged. "I like to get a jump on things when I can."

She took the seat across from Derek, then moved a pancake to her plate. "I wish there was a way I could repay you for all you're doing, but I'm not sure how someone ever returns a favor as big as this. You keep saving my life. Repeatedly."

And she owed more than just Derek. She owed his parents for their acceptance and kindness, the use of all their baby gear and their cabin. She owed Derek's brothers, and the cousin who'd cleaned her home. Their combined generosity was almost too much to process. She'd been a stranger to all of them only a few days ago. Nothing more than a name on the lips of a mutual friend.

"My folks are taking care of the animals for me, and Cruz is helping Dad move Mason's coop and hens later today," he said. "A patrol officer was assigned to check in on your place twice a day."

Allison nodded. All the arrangements had been made. "Sounds like you've got it all covered." Between Blaze's delivery of Allison's and Bonnie's personal items and things borrowed from the Winchesters, they had everything they'd need for at least a week. Though, she'd have to reach out to the day care after that and let them know she wouldn't return from her maternity leave as planned. Her boss would understand, but she'd still need to know why Allison didn't show up. "Do we have time to feed Mason's hens after breakfast?" she asked, sliding the favor she wanted into their conversation as casually as possible. "It's been my job since his heart attack, and I didn't do it yesterday."

"Blaze handled it," Derek said. "He was already there, visiting the crime scene. I realize this is going to sound insane to you, but you don't need to take care of anyone except yourself and Bonnie right now. And here's another wild concept." He smiled broadly and pointed his fork at her. "You aren't alone with her. Understand what I'm saying?" he asked. "People want to be useful. Let them. It feels good for everyone."

Allison shook her head, fighting a returning smile. "So asking for help isn't being rude, lazy or presumptuous?" She hiked one eyebrow. "It's actually me doing someone else a kindness?"

"Exactly," he said, forking a fresh bite of pancake. "Whatever you need. Just ask."

"Okay. So will you take me to Mason's this morning? I'd really like to feed the hens one last time."

Derek smirked. "Clever. Fine. As long as we're quick about it."

She beamed. "A lady could get used to this ask-and-receive business."

"As she should."

Forty minutes later, they loaded the truck with everything they needed for their time at the cabin, then headed to Mason's house.

Allison tucked Bonnie into the sling, then fed the chickens and collected eggs while Derek checked the home for signs of another break-in and kept an eye on the perimeter. It was nice to be back in her old routine, but Mason's absence was palpable, in her heart and in the air.

"You okay?" Derek asked, not for the first time since they'd climbed into Lucas's truck to make the trip.

"Yeah. Just thinking."

"Care to share?" He closed the distance between them in long confident strides, then set steady hands against his hips.

She chewed her lip, deciding where to begin. "I did some research on the missing women last night. I couldn't get their names and faces out of my head." *Bailey, Cari, Genny, Hannah, Lexi, Meg.* "It's like they're haunting me, and I know I have to help them."

He shifted his weight, concern lining his brow. "We talked about that over breakfast. You should focus on you now."

"I know." She was supposed to concentrate on caring for herself and Bonnie, but Derek had also said to ask for help when she needed it, and she definitely needed it. "Maybe you can help me help them," she suggested. "I know we're leaving soon, off to hide in the woods while your brothers chase the bad guys, but hear me out."

He narrowed his eyes.

"I think Cari Fletcher was the woman here with Mason." She pulled her phone from her pocket, then swiped the screen to life. "She's one of the blondes from the flyers Blaze showed us. She's twenty years old and a student at Hanover College in Indiana. The campus website says it's ideally located on the scenic banks of the Ohio River."

Derek moved his attention toward the sound of racing water at the edge of the property. "Is that right?"

"Yep. And," she said, turning her photo to face him, "this is the photo her mom posted on her social media the day Cari went missing."

Derek looked at Allison, then the little screen before him.

"The image in the flyer Blaze had was zoomed in on her face. It said she was wearing jeans and a T-shirt, but look…" She used her fingers to enlarge the photo and bring the sweater folded over Cari's arm into focus. "She had a cardigan with her that day, too. White with small flower-shaped buttons."

"May I?" he asked, reaching for the device.

She released it, ignoring the buzz of electricity as their fingers touched.

Derek tapped the screen several times, then returned the phone to her hand. "I sent a screenshot of that close-up to Blaze, along with a link to the mom's social media."

"Do you think it might've been her?" she asked. "The one who made it here to try to get help?"

"Maybe. The sweater was a good catch," he said. "I kind of hate that I didn't see it."

She laughed. "Were you up researching, too?"

"I was looking through the missing women's profiles for commonalities. Shared friends, groups or frequent stops. I didn't find any connections."

Allison sighed. Derek had stayed awake thinking of the women, too. "I know it sounds ridiculous," she began, "and you've probably been through worse things, but I'm really sorry I dragged you into this. I can't help thinking about how unlucky you were to be there when I crashed. Now you're stuck with me. Indefinitely. You work full-time and run a small business, but you've been pulled away from it for days now, doing something that isn't your job or responsibility. It doesn't seem fair."

Derek frowned. "None of this is fair. Not what happened to Mason. Not what those women are going through, and not what's happening to you. My job is to seek the truth for clients, and my duty is to protect those in need. You and Bonnie are in need."

He was certainly right about that. Allison wasn't able to protect herself properly. That fact had been proven twice, and both times, her daughter had been left alone because of it.

"Mason was right about you," she said. "I should've made an effort to know you sooner."

Derek opened his arms, pulling her easily into a hug. "I'm glad to know you now. And I don't want you to worry. You and Bonnie are going to be okay. That's a promise."

She leaned carefully against his chest, snuggling Bonnie between them and willing the words to be true.

"Mason started telling me about you the moment you came to stay with your grandma," Derek said. "He thought you walked on water."

Allison laughed. "Right now it feels like I'm barely keeping my head above the current."

"How about this then?" he asked, voice low and tender. "I'll be your life raft for a little while, and you can be my anchor."

Her heart melted, and for the first time since they'd met, she knew precisely how much it would hurt when she had to let him go. It wasn't a pain she thought she could manage.

"If it makes you feel any better," he said, broad hands roaming softly over her back, "my family is tougher than we look."

She laughed, stepping back for a look into his warm brown eyes.

"We're smarter, too," he added, one cheek lifting in a charming lopsided smile.

"Well, thank goodness," she said, returning his teasing grin. "I was getting a little worried."

She turned her face to the breeze as it began to blow once more, then took a step toward the river.

DEREK WATCHED AS Allison turned away. He'd joked about his family not being what they seemed, but in reality it was Allison who was so much more. He and his brothers had grown strong with the support of their family, but she'd learned to be strong on her own. And that was a whole other level of strength.

He followed her through the yard on instinct, needing to be where she was.

Allison hadn't had anyone to count on in a long time, and the idea of being that person for her was intoxicating. Knowing she and Bonnie would be gone from his life when the threats against them were contained made him uneasy and unhappy in ways he couldn't explain. And didn't want to.

Thinking of their lives before him made Derek long to punch Bonnie's dad in the nose for being such an idiot. How could anyone who knew Allison ever want to leave? How could someone who'd earned her trust just give it away so easily?

"Care if we walk down to the river before we take off?" she asked, already nearing the yard's edge.

Derek followed without answering, knowing they needed to leave for the cabin, and also that he was incapable of telling her no. He kept his eyes sharp as they moved farther from his truck and closer to the water.

The river was swift and loud, engorged from the recent storms, and climbing higher on the banks than it had since the previous fall.

"Mason and I spent a lot of evenings down here, fishing," Allison said, drawing his eyes back to her. "All he wanted to do after his heart attack was be outside. But he wasn't supposed to do anything. So we negotiated. If he let me push him in the wheelchair, then I'd fish as long as he liked. He carried the poles and tackle box for us, like a gentleman. I'd pack drinks and snacks, and we'd fish until the mosquitoes drove us out."

Derek barked a heavy laugh, the sound breaking unexpectedly from his chest. "I knew all those fish in his freezer were new, and he straight-up lied to me." He shook his head. "Every time I brought casseroles over from Mom, there were more fish. He always swore a friend caught them, but he never wanted to say which friend."

Allison raised her hand. "I mean, to be fair, we both caught our share, but I was his partner in crime. We spent hours talking. He was funny, and an incredible storyteller."

Derek crossed his arms over the ache in his chest.

"I still can't believe he's gone, and I hate that he died while trying to do the right thing," Allison said, as if she'd somehow read Derek's thoughts, yet again. "Worse, the woman he tried to save is no better off now than she was before. It's like her escape and his death was all for nothing."

The wind picked up over the water, throwing Allison's long blond locks across her face and interrupting her words.

Derek squinted against the icy gale, feeling her words and the wind sink deep in his bones. "We can't change what's happened," he said. "But we can help Blaze catch those men and save the women. We can help finish what Mason started."

Another gust of air broke across the water, as the first began to settle.

Allison's hair rose like wings around her face, and Bonnie's floppy hat jerked free from her little head. The pink-and-white checkered bonnet whipped past Derek and floated over the tall grasses along the river.

"Oh!" Allison cried. "Grandma bought her that hat."

Derek was already in motion, tracking the hat as it cartwheeled through weeds and cattails along the river, then stuck to something wedged in the earth. "I've got it."

"Thank you!" Allison called. "Be careful. Look for snakes!"

Derek grinned. "Not my first rodeo," he said, pulling the bonnet free from the snare of a stumpy, rusted metal sign. The long-forgotten marker bore a letter-and-number combination strikingly similar to those on the paper Allison had found.

He pocketed the bonnet, then snapped a photograph of the sign with his phone.

Also caught on the metal, where the bonnet had been, was a length of tangled white yarn.

Possibly from a sweater with flower-shaped buttons.

Chapter Fifteen

Allison waited nervously as Derek chased Bonnie's hat along the riverbank. "Be careful!" she yelled again, projecting her voice above the roaring current.

The rocky riverbank ended abruptly several yards away, and the grasses became tall and bushy. Allison never went anywhere she couldn't see what lurked at her feet. A lifelong fear of snakes made sure of it. One bite from a poisonous snake would do more than ruin someone's day. The venom from some could take lives. Considering that Allison was the only person around to save Derek if he was bitten, the odds of his survival weren't good. She couldn't leave Bonnie behind or risk carrying her into the weeds.

Her hands began to sweat as she watched him. Another "be careful" poised to leap from her tongue.

What if Allison was bitten trying to help him? Or she slipped and fell, then Bonnie was bitten. She curled her arms over her baby, then took a small step backward, away from the weeds. "I hate snakes," she muttered, suppressing a full body shiver.

Derek spun around suddenly, as if he'd somehow

heard her. His eyes were bright as he moved swiftly back in her direction. "Hey," he hollered, waving a hand overhead. "Hang on to these for me. I want to check something out, and I don't want to get them wet." He reached out with his hand when he got near, dropping his cell phone and the key fob to Lucas's truck into her palm.

"What'd you find?" she asked, bracing her back to the wind and curling her shoulders to shelter Bonnie. "Tracks?"

"Yarn," he said, voice and eyebrows rising, as if he wasn't sure. "Take a look at the photos."

The phone was unlocked as she turned her eyes to it. It was tough to make out anything besides the weeds and water.

"Also, here's Bonnie's bonnet." He pulled the hat from his back pocket and passed that to her, as well.

"Thank you." She pocketed the phone, then slipped the gingham accessory over her daughter's wispy soft hair and fastened it under her chin.

"You might have to zoom in on the pictures," he said. "The yarn I found is filthy, but originally white, I think. It could be from the sweater that lost a button inside Mason's house."

Allison grabbed the phone again, examining the image once more.

"I'm going back for the yarn. It's hooked on a rusted post and blowing into the tree line. The rest of the sweater could be at the end."

Yeah, Allison thought nervously, *or the body of the woman wearing it.*

"Lucas keeps plastic evidence bags under the truck seat. We can use those to store the yarn until we get ahold of him or Blaze," Derek said. "One of them can take it to the lab."

"Should I call someone?" she asked, wiggling the phone that no doubt contained contact information for every law-enforcement officer in town.

He frowned. "Give me five minutes to see what I've got."

"Okay," she agreed, hating to see him return to the weeds. "Keep your eyes out for snakes, and watch your step. The muck might pull your boots off." She smiled, hoping to lighten the ominous mood settling over her.

He smirked. "I'll try to keep my boots on."

"That's all I ask." Allison turned her attention to the photo on Derek's phone as he hiked steadily away. Even fully expanded, the yarn he planned to collect was barely visible among the backdrop of weeds and rushing water.

The wind began again, and Allison's muscles went stiff. The faint trace of a familiar scent locked her feet in place. Motor oil? Or perhaps gasoline? Something she associated with car maintenance. Something completely out of place near the woods, weeds and river.

She pocketed Derek's phone, then began a careful scan of the immediate area, scrutinizing the long, flat yard behind her that led to Mason's home. Then she turned her attention on the patch of trees beside the river.

A pair of peculiar shapes came into view a half-dozen yards away. Only feet from where Derek followed the yarn through the weeds. The breeze picked up, and everything around the odd shapes seemed to flutter or bend with its influence. Everything except the shapes that snapped suddenly into focus.

Two ATVs, like the ones she'd seen on the day of Mason's death, had been wrapped in camouflage decals and parked among the trees.

Fear skittered down her spine as she realized the drivers were missing. And the men could be anywhere. Close enough to get the jump on a distracted Derek in seconds. Close enough to succeed in Allison's abduction without Derek having a clue. She reached for her phone, afraid to yell, in case they were near. The phone her fingers found first wasn't hers. It was Derek's.

Her breaths came more quickly as indecision slammed over her. Running to Derek would mean carrying Bonnie closer to the ATVs, possibly closer to the danger. Running for the safety of the truck would be separating from her protector. Leaving him unaware. And neither option was one she could live with.

A tiny movement at the tree line drew her eyes to a man dressed in brown coveralls. He crept forward, eyes fixed on Derek, and approached from his back.

"No!" she screamed. "Derek!"

Bonnie jerked against Allison's middle, startled awake by the sudden sound of her mother's frantic cries.

Derek, on the other hand, turned slowly, brow furrowed, as if he wasn't sure he'd heard her at all.

"There!" she yelled again. "Look!" She clutched Bonnie to her chest, then threw the other arm forward, fingers outstretched toward the trees. "Someone's there!"

Bonnie screamed.

Understanding lit Derek's expression a moment before his head snapped in the direction Allison had pointed.

A heartbeat later, the man leaped from the shadows hugging the bases of the trees. He swung a fallen branch at Derek's head, but received a punch to the gut instead. Derek dodged the blow with lightning reflexes, only to have the doubled-over attacker make a run for Derek's core. The impact threw them both into the river with a splash.

The air sucked from Allison's lungs. The men went under, but they didn't come back up. At least, not anywhere she could see.

And there was another ATV rider somewhere. Unaccounted for.

Her ears rang with fear and the decibel of protests pouring from Bonnie's beet-red face. Bonnie was Allison's top priority. Every day. Everywhere. No matter what.

She spun on her toes and ran back the way she'd come, holding Bonnie close, and trying not to jostle and injure her baby while attempting to save her life. She fished the key to Lucas's truck from her pocket, then pressed the button to unlock the doors when the vehicle came into view.

Her heart wrenched as she threw herself behind the wheel and locked the doors.

Derek was in danger, and she needed to call 911.

She turned on her knees, leaning over the console to transfer Bonnie from her sling to the car seat in back.

Bonnie stiffened her little body in protest. Tears streamed over her bright red cheeks and quivering chin as she wailed.

"Shh," Allison said, voice cracking and shaking as she struggled to secure her baby with the five-point safety harness. "It's okay," she said, as much to herself as Bonnie, relieved by the final click of the buckle.

Allison flipped herself forward. She freed the cell phones from her pocket, dropping Derek's phone into a cup holder. She stuffed herself into the driver's seat, then jammed Lucas's key into the ignition.

She dialed 911 on her cell phone, then hit the speaker button and transferred the device into the second cup holder.

Bonnie's cries ricocheted through the cab, shredding Allison's nerves as the call began to ring. The last time she'd been on the run with her baby, she'd been shot at and crashed her truck.

"West Liberty Dispatch," a woman announced. "What's your location and emergency?"

Allison opened her mouth to respond, but was cut off by the sound of an explosion.

Boom!

Glass shattered behind her, raining into the cab from a hole, newly blown into the rear window.

Allison screamed, and Bonnie screeched.

A look in the rearview mirror revealed a man in a dark coat and jeans moving up the narrow drive behind her, arm extended, gun in hand. Redmon!

Allison jerked the shifter into Drive and stomped the gas pedal. The truck lurched forward, toward the chickens and away from the shooter. Tufts of grass, mud and gravel flew into the air behind her.

She bounded over Mason's property, past the chicken coop and down the path toward the river. She'd briefly considered using Reverse to run over her assailant, but if he got out of the way, the move would provide him with an up-close unmissable shot at her head as she passed.

The truck tore over the soft earth, ripping a path in its wake. The road was behind her, but Redmon had forced her to forge another way. To the river, then around the grove of trees.

In the opposite direction that Derek had disappeared.

"Can you please confirm shots fired?" the dispatcher asked calmly, her voice rising from the forgotten phone in the cup holder.

"Yes," Allison yelled toward the phone. "This is Allison Hill. There's an active shooter at Mason Montgomery's property on River Road. Send help. Tell them Derek Winchester was attacked. He and the man who jumped him are in the river."

A figure suddenly appeared on her right, outside the passenger window.

She jammed on the brakes, recognizing Derek on instinct, even before she could make out his features in the stress of her situation. "Get in!" she screamed, pressing the button on her door to unlock the truck for Derek.

He threw himself inside. Water dripped from his clothes and nose. His drenched hair was plastered to his head and clung to his forehead. "Go!" he hollered, pointing back the way she'd come.

"I can't. There's a shooter!"

His eyes widened a fraction, as he seemed to realize for the first time that Allison wasn't driving the truck across the lawn for kicks, or even to save him. She was running for her life. And Bonnie's.

The sound of a racing ATV pulled her attention outside the truck once more. Redmon was now on one of the vehicles she'd seen parked among the trees, and he was coming for them, gun in hand.

Bonnie's anguished screams pierced Allison's heart.

She had to get her baby to safety. "What do I do?"

"Hit him."

Derek's body jerked forward as Allison yanked the wheel in the ATV's direction and smashed the gas pedal with her foot.

The ATV charged forward, but Redmon didn't shoot. He seemed determined to get in front of her. Perhaps to stop her escape.

The front bumper of Lucas's truck clipped the rear tire of the four-wheeler, and it swerved wildly.

Allison sank low in the seat, in case he changed his mind about pulling the trigger, then pressed the gas harder as the ATV regained control and came for her again. Instead of attempting to stop her now, he raised the gun to shoot her.

The impact of their second collision was severe.

As much as she didn't want to hurt the man, not even when he so adamantly wanted to get his hands on her, she could not allow him to further endanger her baby. She'd taken Derek's advice, and would have to deal with the consequences later.

Redmon went airborne.

And the ATV rolled roughly before splashing into the river.

Chapter Sixteen

Derek paced the riverbank—he was cold, wet and angry. He'd been ambushed, and he was better than that. Or at least, he was supposed to be. Two decades of combined military training and PI experience, plus a lifetime of hunting, should have taught him to be alert and never let down his guard. Especially when he was somewhere trouble could hide. Like beside a grove of trees.

Frustration and humiliation roiled in him, sparking his temper and destroying his mood. He'd been so enraptured with the unexpected length of yarn, so certain the small clue would blow the case wide open, that he'd forgotten himself, and the handful of minutes it'd taken him to collect the potential evidence had nearly cost him everything. The shame and guilt of failing so miserably at something so basic was unfathomable. Worse, he'd allowed Allison and Bonnie to be ambushed, too. And that was unforgivable.

He stared at the fateful spot, several yards downstream, where he'd dragged his unconscious attacker ashore after knocking him out cold in the water.

The stone-and-mud riverbank was empty now. The son of a gun was gone, along with the ATV Derek had spotted in the trees as he'd raced back to Allison.

The sound of a gunshot had stopped his heart. He'd thought he'd lost her, but once again, no thanks to him, she'd prevailed.

He rubbed a heavy hand across his forehead, watching a set of cops in waders attempting to recover the overturned ATV from the water. Redmon Firth, the rat who'd flown off the vehicle after Allison ran into it with Lucas's truck was nowhere to be found.

He glanced in the direction of the ambulance, where she and Bonnie were being given a thorough once-over by Isaac. He hated how badly he'd let down Allison.

He hadn't even been sure he'd heard her voice when he'd turned to look for her. It was more instinct than auditory response. Then, he'd seen her face, and registered the sheer terror as she'd yelled and pointed into the shadows along the trees.

"Hey, Winchester," Isaac called, making his way in Derek's direction, a medical kit in one hand.

Derek frowned. "I'm fine."

"I'll be the judge of that." His cousin stopped a few feet away and dragged his keen gaze from Derek's sopping-wet hair to his soaked-through boots. "You look like hell."

"Yeah." He turned his attention back to the cops

guiding the ATV from the river. "You should've seen the other guy."

Isaac smiled, already opening his kit. "I wish I could see him. Any ideas where he went?"

"Nope."

That was the problem. No one knew where to find either of these two psychos.

Isaac moved efficiently around Derek, cleaning and bandaging the worst of the scrapes and cuts on Derek's face, neck and arms. When he finished with that, he flashed a light into his eyes.

Derek pushed it away. "Knock it off."

"Any dizziness, nausea, vomiting?" Isaac asked, dropping the light back into his pocket. "Pain in your head or neck?"

"Not until you walked over here," Derek said, softening the retort with a grin. "Now I'm experiencing a little of both."

"I see your sense of humor is weak as ever."

"How are Allison and Bonnie?" Derek asked, casting a cautious gaze in the ladies' direction. Obviously, neither of them needed emergency treatment, or Isaac would've insisted on taking them immediately. But it would be reassuring to hear him say it.

Isaac's expression softened. "I'm more concerned about you right now." He stole a look at Derek as he began to repack his medical gear. "You've always been independent. Overconfident. And, more recently, a loner. I don't agree with your reasoning on that, but we both know the cause. Now you've got a lady and a baby to look after. Two untrained partners of sorts. Danger keeps coming for them, and the criminals are getting past you on occasion. It's a lot of complicated similarities to that thing you never talk about."

"When I was a cop." Derek ground out the words. "And Terrance died."

Isaac rocked back on his heels. "You see the symmetry, and you said his name. I feel like this is what the counseling crowd would call a breakthrough." He dabbed something cold against a cut on Derek's cheek, and Derek hissed in response. "Be still," Isaac warned. "You don't want whatever's living in the river to grow on your face."

"I'm fine," Derek said, shrugging away his cousin. "Thank you for the bandages and concern."

"I pester because I care. Also because you'll regret a river-water infection. If you ever need to talk…" He raised a palm, then let it drop.

"Yeah. I know."

Isaac always meant well, but Derek wasn't a talker. He was a worker, and right now, he needed something to do.

A slamming door made him turn around. He scanned the property, which was crawling with law enforcement, in search of the sound.

Isaac chuckled as Lucas came into view.

"What the hell, man?" Lucas hollered, expression grim as he rounded the side of Derek's pickup.

Allison waved as he stormed past.

"Someone shot my truck!" Lucas stretched a hand in the direction of his battered pickup. "And the front end is all messed up. You haven't had the keys for twenty-four hours."

Derek grinned, enjoying his younger brother's ruffled feathers. "How was Louisville?"

Lucas stopped a few feet away and dug the fingers of both hands into his overgrown hair. "Great."

"Insurance will cover the damage," Isaac said. "But I'm a strong proponent of 'turnabout is fair play.' So maybe shooting Derek's truck will make you feel better."

Lucas looked over his shoulder, toward the trucks.

"Don't even think about it," Derek said.

Lucas laughed. "Fine. Steal my fun." He turned cool blue eyes on Isaac. "Big brother needs a new ride now. The killers have seen him in mine."

"I doubt he wants my hybrid sedan," Isaac said flatly.

"Accurate," Derek agreed.

"Well, my pickup is headed to the shop." Lucas waved a hand at the roughed-up pickup. "I've got to have the window replaced and get a price on the body work for my insurance company. What are you going to drive now?"

Blaze moved swiftly in their direction. "You can't have my truck," he called, either overhearing or predicting their conversation. "But I need an official statement from you. Preferably in writing." He stopped at Derek's side and handed him a dry T-shirt, then a pad of paper and pen. "Allison already gave hers."

Derek accepted the T-shirt, but waved off the rest.

"Can I email something when I get home?" He discarded the wet shirt, then pulled the dry one over his frozen, pebbled skin and rubbed the spot on his chest where an ache had begun to grow.

"Yeah, but this afternoon, if you can. Before you head up to the cabin."

Derek nodded his agreement.

"How's it going with Allison?" Blaze asked, lowering his voice enough to let the group know he wasn't speaking professionally. This was brother talk. "She seems pretty great. Kid's adorable. How are the two of you getting along?" He shot a conspiratorial look at the other men in the circle.

"We're getting along just fine, if you ignore the fact that someone's constantly trying to kill her, and I'm close to losing my damn mind."

His brothers smiled.

Allison appeared then, only a few feet away. She had a deep frown in place and Bonnie in tow. "Sorry. I didn't think I would be interrupting. I was over there alone, and it looked like you guys might be discussing something I could get in on."

Derek groaned internally, then slid a palm against the unshaven column of his throat. "You're not interrupting. Come on over. How are you both feeling?"

"Good." She pressed her lips together, dropping her gaze to her feet before lifting it back to Derek. "How about you?"

"Good."

She pulled in a long breath as Bonnie began to fuss, then turned her forced smile on Blaze. "Any luck finding or tracking the men who were here today?"

"Afraid not, but the ATV they left behind will help. Someone had to buy it," he said.

Allison nodded. "You can trace the vehicle through registration?"

"Sort of," Blaze said. "ATVs don't legally need to be registered in Kentucky, but they are required to be titled. We should be able to find the owner that way."

"That's perfect. Will it take long?"

"No. We just have to hope the vehicle wasn't stolen. How did it go for you with the criminal database last night?" he asked. "Were you able to identify the other man?"

"No, but it was the same guy with Redmon again today," Allison said.

Derek shifted. "I got a good look at both men this time. Maybe I can help with the database."

"You'll have to be quick," Blaze said. "I still need that statement, and you should try to get to the cabin before dark. There's no internet up there. Cell reception is spotty, but existent."

Bonnie gave a soft cry, and Allison adjusted her in the sling once more, working to quiet her with cuddles and soft shushes.

"I'm going to text Cruz," Derek said. "His Jeep is perfect for the trip to the cabin, and he can watch my house while I'm gone. He's good with the animals, and he loves my truck."

Allison handed Lucas the key to his pickup, then freed Bonnie from the sling when she continued to fuss.

"Here." Derek stepped into the center of their little group, reaching for Bonnie as she began to cry. "I've got her. What do you need?"

Allison accepted his help with a look of complete relief. "I'll run and grab her bottle. It's past time for that."

Derek adjusted the tiny human in his arms, then jostled her gently while Allison went after the diaper bag.

Bonnie stilled, seeming to realize she'd been passed to someone new. She blinked big blue eyes, then sucked in a shuddered breath and worked her tiny mouth in circles. Maybe planning to cry again. Maybe desperate for her bottle. Derek wasn't sure, but he was entranced.

His brothers openly gaped. Derek pointedly ignored them.

"Try this," Allison said, rushing back and shaking a bottle as she ran.

He accepted the offering, then tipped the clear spongy nipple to Bonnie's mouth.

Allison watched curiously for a moment—maybe she was thinking of taking back her baby, maybe testing out what it felt like to get help when she needed it. Eventually, she stuffed her fingers into the back pockets of her jeans, then dragged her attention to Blaze. "Were you able to get a match on the blood and hair from Mason's house? And did they belong to Cari Fletcher, by chance?"

Blaze crossed his arms and widened his stance,

apparently both amused and taken aback by her correct assumption. "Yes, but how did you know that?"

"The sweater in her photo."

Blaze nodded. "That was smart work."

A nonsensical swell of pride rose in Derek's chest. He had to work to keep his eyes fixed on Bonnie.

"Have you learned anything about the teenager who disappeared last night?" she asked, a measure of maternal concern in her voice. "Can you tell me her name?"

"Zoey Walls. She's a senior in high school, honors student, band member. We can't find anything to suggest she might be a runaway." Blaze swept his gaze over the group. "My gut says she was snatched by the same men we're looking for. If not them specifically, then others in the same group."

Allison wrapped her arms around herself, brow furrowed as she considered the information. "I looked into the social-media accounts for the six women on the flyers you brought with you last night," she said. "They're all blondes, from platinum to dishwater, but nothing darker. Do you think it's a coincidence, or the abductors have a type? And if someone's collecting blondes, then where does the black hair you found fit in?"

Blaze shook his head. "I can't say. Could be that we're only looking at a small piece of a big picture."

Allison deflated a bit. "The online posts from their families and friends are heartbreaking. They're all missed very much."

"Yeah." Lucas offered a sad smile. "I touch base

with their families as often as I can. Even if I don't have anything new to share. We don't forget or give up on anyone in this county. I try to make sure they know."

Derek passed Allison the empty bottle, savoring the quiet exchange between then. She fit so well with his family. And in his life. He'd like to make more memories with her and with Bonnie. New ones. Better ones.

He turned Bonnie against his chest, the way he'd seen Allison do so many times before, then patted her narrow back.

He was definitely losing his edge. And his damn mind.

So, why did it feel so good?

Chapter Seventeen

The drive back to Derek's house was quiet. Allison
was completely spent from another emotional morning, and Bonnie had fallen asleep after her bottle. Allison would never stop counting her lucky stars that
Bonnie was completely unharmed when a window
had shattered just inches from her car seat. Despite
the bad things happening lately, her little family of
two was miraculously well. And beginning to feel
more like a family of three.

They left Derek's truck in the driveway, then
marched solemnly inside.

Allison settled Bonnie in the crib and grabbed the
speaker before returning to the living room, where
Derek was waiting. "We should probably talk before
we run off into the wilderness together," she said,
hoping to sound lighter than she felt.

Derek turned guarded eyes on her, moving his
attention from the front window to where she stood
behind him. Anguish played on his handsome features, and she recognized the guilt and shame there.

"What happened today wasn't your fault," she

said. "No more than any of the rest. These guys are following us. They're lurking, and they're waiting. Which is why we're leaving. But what's important is that we keep beating them at their games."

The muscles of his square jaw flexed, but he didn't speak.

"Anyway," she said, working up a pleasant smile. "Tell me about this cabin."

"It belongs to my family," he said. "My grandfather built it when my dad was young, and we've been using it for vacations and hunting for decades. Mom made sure there was electricity and running water years ago. Local gas and logging companies have popped up in the area, and cell-phone towers followed, so there's service. We'll stay in communication with Blaze and Lucas. We have movies on disc, board games, food and amazing views. No internet, but otherwise, we can do anything there that we can do here. The venue is just significantly more private."

Allison felt her cheeks flush as images of things she'd like to do privately with Derek paraded through her mind. "And is it far?"

"It's about an hour. Only twenty miles or so, but the speed limits there are low, and the drive up the mountain can be painstaking. Though it should be easier with Cruz's Jeep," he explained.

"Okay." She folded her hands in front of her, attempting to look more casual than she felt, while staring up at the man who'd become her constant savior. A man who was also slowly stealing her heart. "Do you think we should talk about anything before we go isolate ourselves together for an undetermined amount of time?"

His deep brown eyes turned curious. "Like what?"

"Well, for starters," she began, forcing the awkward words past her lips, "sometimes I feel as if there's something between us." She paused to fight the urge to abandon her mission. This needed to be said before she went off to play house with him. She needed to know if she imagined the toe-curling chemistry. Or if she was alone in this, too. "It's just a feeling," she continued, "but it's a struggle to ignore, for me, anyway. And last night there was a moment when I thought you might've felt it, too."

She bit her lip and waited, determined to simply get her answer, then deal with it. Even if it was a rejection that made her want to dig a hole and hide under the cabin.

His gaze darkened as he scanned her face, an internal battle thinly veiled behind those deep brown eyes. "Now that you mention it, there was a moment when I thought you were going to kiss me," he said, a twitch of humor in his cheeks.

Relief rushed through her. He hadn't denied it. And she wasn't crazy. Or so desperately lonely that she'd begun imagining connections that weren't there. "You were going to kiss me," she corrected. "I was deciding what to do about it."

"Did you get that figured out?"

A smile split her face, uncontrollable and easy. "Not really," she admitted.

"Shame," he said. "But for now, I'm going to double down on my goal, which is to protect you and Bonnie."

"Honorable." She offered her hand for a shake, and bit her lip again when he accepted, encasing her small soft fingers in his larger, stronger ones.

"I won't fail you," he vowed.

"I know."

Motion outside the window drew their attention and broke the spell between them.

A white Jeep barreled down the gravel lane.

"Cruz is here," Derek said, releasing her hand and stepping away. "We're square?"

"Yeah. Good talk." Her cheeks ached with a smile she was powerless to stop, and she nearly collapsed with relief as he walked away.

DEREK MET HIS cousin outside, then transferred all their luggage once more. This time into the back of the Jeep.

"I hear you've had a wild day," Cruz said, handing over his keys when the work was done. "It's only noon. Any chance you were followed here?"

"I don't think so." Derek shook his head, still disgusted with the way everything had gone down. "The record I'm keeping lately, they might be inside the house right now, and I wouldn't know."

Cruz didn't bother to tell him he was wrong, like his brothers had. It was one of the reasons they worked so well at the PI firm. They were partners, and knew how to leave one another alone unless asked.

Derek tossed the bags into the Jeep, frustration

and desperation curling in him. "The shooter could have hit Allison or Bonnie. And I wasn't there to protect them. Because I was wrestling with some chump who got the drop on me."

"But they're fine," Cruz said. "And the way I understand it, that little run-in turned up a five-hundred-pound piece of evidence, so it was hardly all for nothing."

Derek stopped to stare at his partner. "Who told you about the ATV?" He'd planned to let Allison fill in Cruz on her hit-and-run that saved the day.

"West Liberty's finest, of course." Cruz smiled a broad, perfect smile, squinting slightly against the sun. "Guess who has been officially tasked to run down that four-wheeler's owner for the local police department?"

"Blaze hired us for that?" Derek asked, not sure why he was so surprised. It would be an easy enough task, and take the busywork off Blaze's plate, so he could focus on whatever else he had to look into. Derek was already elbows deep in the case, so he supposed it made sense to keep the details in-house. "Do you have time?" he asked, following his first question with another.

"Yes and yes," Cruz said. "Most of my cases are research right now. I can work from anywhere, including your place for the next few days or so." He pulled a worn green military duffel from his back seat, then slung it over his shoulder. "I'm tailing a potentially cheating spouse on Friday night, but aside from that, you'll find me right here. Drinking your whiskey and enjoying your views."

"Great." Derek cast him a sideways glance as they reached the porch steps. "Enjoy. But stay out of my whiskey."

Cruz laughed, but didn't agree to the terms.

The front door swung open, and Allison smiled in welcome. "Hi, Cruz."

"Allison," he returned. "I hear you've been busy today."

She snorted. "Well, I try," she said, stepping aside to let them in. "I'm not feeling truly productive until I've hit someone with a truck before lunch."

"Productivity is the key to happiness," Cruz said, tossing his bag onto the floor. "What are you working on now?" He lifted his chin in the direction of Blaze's open laptop on the kitchen island, not missing a beat.

"I'm trying to find the mug shot of the second attacker."

Derek's stomach growled, and he pressed a palm against the pang of hunger. "How about some sandwiches before we hit the road?"

"Sure. Need some help?" Allison asked.

"I've got it." He pulled ham and cheese from the fridge, then grabbed bread from the pantry.

Behind him, Cruz and Allison fell into a recap of the morning's events.

Allison's words were rushed as she provided the play-by-play. "It was awful. And I don't know how he did it, but Derek knocked the guy out while being swept down river. I mean, how is that even possible?" The touch of awe in her tone drew his eyes to her, as a senseless measure of pride wiggled in his chest.

Cruz smirked, catching the private exchange. "He's always been a wily one."

Derek turned back to the lunch prep, eager to hear what else Allison might say.

"Then he swam to shore, towing the first guy. And if Redmon, that's the second guy, hadn't been shooting at me, Derek could've brought his guy in. Instead, he ran all the way back to where we started and got in the truck with Bonnie and me. By the time the dust settled, both men had vanished, and we still don't know the first guy's identity."

Derek cut the sandwiches in halves, then ferried the plates to the island. "I didn't even get the damn string I went after. I barely had it collected before I was blindsided."

Cruz went straight for the dill spear on his plate and bit in. "Doesn't matter. You got the ATV. That's better. I can trace it."

"Maybe," Derek replied, hoping for the best, but knowing the vehicle could've been stolen. "Did you hear about the sign?"

Allison paused, then asked, "What sign?"

Cruz moved on to his sandwich. "No."

Derek described the rusted metal pole hidden among the weeds. "I think it was one of the old mile markers set up in this area to identify stops and help gauge distance. They were popular before farms and small businesses lined the shores. Boats needed some way to determine where they were along the long stretch between ports. Dad used to point them out on our insane canoe trips, but they were never so close to home."

Allison hung on each word, seeming to forget her sandwich. "What if there are more of those left than you think?"

Derek pulled his phone from his pocket. "I wondered the same thing. If those numbers are part of the code scribbled on the paper you found, it would explain why Blaze and his team are having so much trouble making heads or tails of it." He scrolled through his photos, searching for the image of the paper.

Allison smiled, excitement rising in her features.

"Maybe that ATV wasn't the only big lead to come out of y'all's morning adventure," Cruz said. He set his phone on the counter, then dialed Blaze on speaker and explained the theory.

Derek finished his sandwich while he listened.

"I like it," Blaze agreed when Cruz finished talking. "Part of the pattern looks like dates and times, but I wasn't sure about the rest. I'd assumed the other markings had to do with money."

Allison leaned on the counter in the phone's direction. "What if Cari Fletcher got her hands on the information, then escaped with the list to try to save the other women? You might have the date, time and location of their next stop."

Derek nodded. It was possible. "It would explain why they've been lingering when they could've been long gone days ago," he added.

"They're on a schedule," Blaze said.

Derek's positive vibes shattered with thoughts of the teen who disappeared the day before. "And they might've had one more girl to get."

Chapter Eighteen

Derek pulled out of his driveway, keeping careful watch on their surroundings. It was nearly three in the afternoon and far later than he'd intended to start for the cabin, but he'd stopped to send the promised written statement by email to Blaze. Then a series of messages on the case had kept them glued to their phones and guessing what might happen next.

After they'd determined the old river markers could play a role in the code everyone had been working on, Blaze called back to say one of the ATVs had left some oil in the trees where they'd been parked, along with bits of broken fender, suggesting one of his or Officer Flint's shots had hit the vehicle as it raced away from Allison's home two days before.

Allison confirmed smelling the spilled oil at some point before seeing the vehicles and the first rider, and they'd disconnected expecting that to be the end for a while.

Instead, Derek's phone had rung again as Allison strapped Bonnie into her car seat. Blaze called to say a man fitting Redmon's description had shown up at a clinic near the Bellemont College campus, claiming to have fallen from a deer stand. Blaze had already spread word of the two assailants to every medical facility in the county. And, given the fact that it was nowhere near deer season, and the man was soaked to the bone after his unintentional swim in the river, the intake nurse had called Dispatch to report the patient.

Blaze was on his way to the clinic now, and would call when he could confirm the man as Allison's continued assailant. He was earning gold today for keeping them in the loop.

Derek's muscles itched as he drove—he was eager to get out there and help hunt. To wade into the trenches with his brothers, and work. The sleepy baby and remarkable woman beside him were the only things strong enough to hold him in place.

"Do you think Redmon would really go to a clinic for help?" Allison asked. "He must know the police are watching for him."

"It's possible," he said. "Depends how badly he was hurt and how desperate he was for treatment. He took a heavy hit on that ATV, and he lost his ride. He had to walk to the clinic. If he went in the water with his cell phone, he wouldn't have a way to call for a pickup."

"On foot and in pain," Allison said. "I guess desperate times do call for desperate measures."

"He couldn't even call a Lyft," Derek said, feeling his smile grow. "He could've broken something.

Could have a concussion. He's lucky he was able to get up and move at all."

She kneaded her hands on her lap, her expression torn. "Is it stupid that I hope he isn't hurt too badly? Even after what he's done?"

"No." Derek stole a glance at her as he took the next turn out of town. "It makes you kind. You'd rather see him punished in the courts like a criminal, than broken or beaten like an animal. That's incredibly gracious of you. You're a decent human. He's the monster."

Allison's lips curled slightly. "Thanks. I think that's one of the longest speeches I've heard you give."

"I can be wordy when it comes to the things I feel strongly about."

"Like the law?" she asked, a flirtatious expression growing on her beautiful face. "Due process and all that?"

"Yeah." He flicked his eyes to her briefly. "I'm incredibly passionate about our court system."

"Would you have hit him with the truck?" she asked, her tone going soft and serious again. "If you'd been driving?"

Derek snorted. "I'd have run him flat over."

She laughed, and the knot of tension in Derek's chest eased by a fraction.

He wasn't sure he was kidding, but he was glad to have lightened her mood. "You were brave to do what you did, and I know it wasn't easy for you," he said. "But those injuries you caused might be what leads the cops to Mason's killer and returns all those missing women."

Allison picked at the cuff of her sweatshirt, gaze bouncing from the invisible lint to the window at her side. "If it is Redmon at the clinic, I don't think he'll talk. He seemed sincerely afraid of someone. If he believed it would be better to be caught than to return without me, I can't see him saying anything to Blaze that will help the case. It feels like this potential breakthrough is just going to be another dead end."

"Hey." Derek reached for her hand and squeezed. "It's going to work out."

"What if he doesn't talk?" she asked.

"He'll talk," Derek assured her. "Everyone has a weakness. Even the folks who seem to have nothing to lose. And Blaze deals with people like that all the time. He speaks their language. He'll figure it out."

She released his hand, eyes still on the window, watching fields and farms grow farther and farther apart. "I wish I would've been able to find the other guy in the database."

"Me, too," he admitted, "but what's important now is that we get to the cabin without incident and stay until we hear it's safe to leave. Hopefully that won't be too long. Cruz will track the ATV back to the owner by its title, and whoever that is will be linked to these guys one way or another. Even if it was a shady online transaction, or a person-to-person one, every thread leads to another, and you've got a crew of badass Winchesters on the case."

She laughed. "Okay. You're right. I need to let this go and wait for Blaze to call."

"And you know he'll call," Derek said. He gave her another long look. Her knees bobbed violently, and her hands fidgeted against her lap. "Are you anxious about staying at the cabin?"

"A little. I've never stayed in a cabin. I've slept in tents and the bed of a pickup truck, but never in a cabin in the woods. I'll be fine as long as there aren't any snakes."

Derek forced a tight smile, instantly disliking whomever she'd shared a tent or pickup bed with. "No snakes," he promised.

Allison twisted for a peek into the back seat, where Bonnie slept. "I wish she didn't have to go through all this."

"You'll protect her," he said. "Like you always do."

"I hope so." Allison turned back with a worry-filled sigh. "Tell me about how you and Cruz came to open the private-investigations firm together. Were you always the Winchesters who went their own way?"

"Kind of," he admitted. "Growing up, everyone else wanted to play cops and robbers. I wanted to be left alone to ride my horse. Cruz wanted to play ball. He could hit a crab apple with a stick into the next county before he could write his name."

"Impressive. Did he play college ball?"

"No. His mama got sick his senior year of high school. He wouldn't leave her side, so he missed most of baseball season. The scouts quit calling. He didn't care. That was never what was most important to him."

"I'm so sorry," she said. "I had no idea."

"It's not something he talks about," Derek said, slowing at the private road to the cabin. "But the bottom line is that family comes first. Always and no matter what the personal cost."

ALLISON ABSORBED THE beauty before her with stark appreciation. She'd lived in Kentucky all her life, but she'd never been in the mountains. Not like this. She'd driven past them. Even hiked a few wooded trails. But this was a whole other level of wonderful.

Cruz's Jeep dug its knobby tires into the narrow, pitted lane and growled its way up a never-ending incline. A hill covered in leaves and trees rose on one side. A cliff plummeted sharply on the other.

Bonnie stirred behind them as they bumped along the road to an eventual expanse of flat land atop the mountain. A deep brown log cabin sat at the center of a grassy patch, with a stone chimney climbing one side.

"Is that a wraparound porch?" she asked, unfastening her seat belt and reaching for the door.

"Yeah. There's a firepit on the other side. Mama keeps a set of rocking chairs for the porch and a half-dozen pop-up seats for enjoying the campfire."

Allison climbed out, stretching her legs and inhaling the sweet mountain air.

Derek ejected Bonnie's car seat, then carried her around to Allison. "Ready for the two-cent tour?"

"Absolutely."

Derek led the way into the cabin. Round stones, like the ones she'd seen on the chimney outside, covered the fireplace from floor to ceiling. Slabs of slate made up the hearth. And a mantel of reclaimed wood held photos of Derek and his brothers in their youth.

A sofa, chair and coffee table were arranged to face the fire. Area rugs in warm earthy tones anchored the furniture, and small accents of black bears, deer and other wildlife punctuated the decor.

"Living room," he said. "Kitchen."

She turned to follow his lead. A small L-shaped set of cabinets was bookended by a refrigerator and stove. A sink was situated beneath a window that overlooked the Jeep parked outside. A table with four chairs stood on another rug, visually dividing the rooms.

"One bathroom." Derek flipped the light switch inside a tiny closet of a room off the kitchen, complete with toilet, shower stall and sink. More earth tones, wildlife statues and a throw rug that nearly covered the entire floor.

"Two bedrooms." He moved several steps down the hallway and opened his arms, indicating the doors on either side.

The first room had a matching bed, nightstand and dresser. The second had a folded cot and set of bunkbeds.

Derek grimaced at the latter. "I'll take the couch."

Allison didn't blame him. The cot looked miserable, even without opening it. And Derek was easily six inches too long for the homemade bunkbeds. "Bonnie and I can take this room," she said. "You gave up your bed last time. It's my turn to make a couple sacrifices."

"Being removed from your home and forced into mountaintop isolation with me isn't enough punishment for you?"

She bit into her lip as his gaze caught hers, and the familiar buzz of electricity started between them. "Being with you isn't a sacrifice."

His expression strained briefly before he seemed to regain himself. "Why don't I build a fire while you get familiar with the place. We can fight over who gets the worst sleeping arrangements later."

Allison agreed, then helped set up Bonnie's borrowed baby gear and put away their things as Derek carried them in from the Jeep. He sent messages to his family, letting everyone know they'd arrived safely, and his parents responded with photos of Clark wearing one of his father's ties. Lucas and Blaze reminded him to text if he or Allison needed anything. Cruz sent a photo of Derek's whiskey. She wasn't sure what it meant, but it made Derek laugh, and for that, she was grateful.

The rest of the day passed without incident. And between the occasional bouts of awkward and hard-to-ignore chemistry, there were moments of perfectly companionable silence she wished would last forever.

Sometimes, when she caught Derek looking at her, she thought he might feel that way, too.

Chapter Nineteen

Derek paced the porch as the sun began to set, sending up silent prayers for information from his brothers as he checked his phone for the thousandth time. There was too much radio silence, and he didn't like it. What were they doing? What progress was being made? What setbacks had they encountered? Why wasn't Blaze blowing up his phone now, the way he had been earlier?

He walked the aged boards, hands on hips, eyes set on the dimming daylight, burning orange and apricot through the trees. Derek hated to be taken out of play at a time like this, and the job of sitting and waiting was beginning to make him stir-crazy. It had only been a few hours. What would he be like two days from now? Three?

"Derek?" Allison stepped onto the porch beside him, a long cardigan wrapped around her narrow frame and crisscrossed over her chest. Soft blond hair fell over her shoulders as she curled in on herself.

He moved instantly to her side. "Cold?" He lifted his arms and she unfurled, pressing every inch of herself against every inch of him.

"Thanks," she whispered. "Any word from Blaze?"

"Nothing from him yet." He wrapped her up gently, cradling and comforting her, sliding his hands against her back and keeping her near. "Is Bonnie sleeping?"

"Yeah. I set the monitor on the kitchen table, though I don't think I'll need it. This place is small like mine. If she needs me, I'll know."

Derek absorbed Allison's warmth, thinking about her words. The connections people developed were strange. He supposed she would call them cosmic or something equally inexplicable. Before her, he would've disagreed, but something had spoken to him on the riverbank, as he'd collected the yarn. A sense of panic had overcome him. And he'd turned to see her face. He'd known then that it was too late. Whatever danger he'd sensed had already been upon them.

He wouldn't let the same thing happen again.

"I thought I heard the phone ring," she said, tightening her grip on him when he began to relax the embrace.

He smiled and reciprocated the squeeze. "That was Lucas. He wanted us to know he hasn't gotten back to us sooner because the guy at the clinic was Redmon, and he's not talking. Blaze and the chief have been pushing him for information all day." Just like Allison had predicted.

"Was he badly hurt?" she asked, a thread of guilt in her voice.

"Three broken ribs and a fractured clavicle."

She was quiet, maybe processing how she felt about hurting another human being. He wasn't sure, but he was more than ready to defend her actions again, and as many times as she needed. Much too soon, she pulled away. "What about Cruz and the ATV title?"

"I don't know." Derek rested his head on hers. Cruz was generally quick when it came to digging up details, especially easily accessible ones like those found in title searches. And he was usually better at communication.

Allison stepped out of his embrace, and they watched one another for a long and palpable moment. Worry lined her brow and tugged at the corners of her mouth.

He longed to erase her concern and the small space between them. Ached to hold her after he'd just let her go. It wasn't normal how badly he wanted her, or how often he thought of having her in his life, long after the danger had passed.

For now, he reminded himself. *There was only one job to do. Keep her and Bonnie safe.* Whatever the cost.

"Do you think there's a chance something bad happened to Cruz?" she asked. "Could that be why he hasn't called?"

Derek shook his head, confident in his answer. "Unlikely. Cruz is tough and he's cunning. Anyone who's ever been lucky enough to get the drop on him hasn't had it for long, and they were all sorry in the end."

Allison hugged herself again. "So why isn't he calling?"

"I'm sure there's a good reason." Derek opened the cabin door, and offered her a hand. "How about a cup of hot tea?" he suggested, brimming with satisfaction when she set her narrow palm over his.

Derek set the kettle on to boil, and Allison took a seat at the table, legs crossed and knee bobbing.

He wasn't sure what had her so keyed up, but her eyes continued to drift his way, as if he might know the answer to her troubles.

He racked his mind with ways to put her at ease and failed miserably. Then he remembered the first day they'd met. She'd eaten ice cream for comfort. The cabin didn't have ice cream, but maybe there was another option.

His phone buzzed with an incoming text, and Allison jolted to her feet. "It's Cruz."

Allison met Derek at the stove and read the text with him. "He did it." She sighed and leaned against him.

"He did it," Derek echoed.

Cruz traced the ATV title to a woman in Louisville named Lonnie Vox. Lonnie had a lengthy record of passing bad checks and fraud. She also had two warrants out for her arrest. And one domestic-violence incident several years back involving a longtime boyfriend and serial rapist, George Lanier.

Derek swept his arm around her, pulling her close as they continued to read the incoming texts.

George was a violent repeat offender with a lifetime spent in and out of juvenile detention centers for hurting people, usually women, and eventually he'd gone to prison. He'd been released from the state's supermax facility ninety days back, when a technicality overturned his most recent conviction. Roughly three weeks before the first woman from Blaze's stack of missing-person flyers went missing.

The next message that appeared was from Blaze, and it was short and to the point.

Made a trade with Lonnie. Erasing her warrants in exchange for information leading to George's location. On our way there now.

Allison squeaked. "This is amazing!" She covered her mouth with trembling fingertips and stole a look in the direction of the baby monitor. When Bonnie didn't stir, Allison released a sigh. "Now what?"

"Now we wait to hear that Blaze has George in custody," Derek said.

The kettle whistled, and Derek stepped away. He pulled it from the stove before it could wake the baby, then filled two mugs with steaming water and added a tea bag to each. He delivered the mugs to the table, then made another trip to pick up a box of sugar packets his mother kept in the cupboard for her coffee. It reminded him of his quest for something sweet to share with Allison.

She eagerly ripped the tops off two paper packets and dumped the crystals into her mug. "Do you think George will be with the women?" she asked. "Then Blaze can free them when he arrests George."

Derek took the seat at her side. "I'm not sure. Lucas will likely take the lead from here, or work side by side with Blaze moving forward. Lucas has informants and connections in that world who might become useful now. Meanwhile, we just sit tight."

"Right." She lifted the mug to her lips with shaky hands. "I don't know how to feel," she said, setting down the cup a moment later with a clatter. "I'm feeling a little bit of everything. From relief for the lead that panned out, to fear for the women who aren't yet safe. I'm thrilled things are finally going our way and terrified something horrible is about to go wrong."

"There's still a lot of unknowns," Derek agreed. "It can be hard to turn off our minds." And he had some worries of his own. Like what if Blaze was too late, and George had already taken the women and moved on. Or if Lonnie had given him bad information to buy time. "I think the best thing we can do now is try to keep our minds off all the what-ifs."

Allison raised her mug to her lips again, looking a little flushed. "What do you have in mind?"

The phone buzzed again, and he flipped it over in his palm, thankful he hadn't had time to ponder that question.

"Fingers crossed for more good news," she said, leaning in for a look at the small screen's display.

A photograph of George in handcuffs appeared seconds after two precious words.

Got him.

Allison threw her arms around Derek's neck, then kissed his cheek. Her eyes were bright and glistening with unshed tears when she pulled herself away. "What about the women?"

Derek texted Blaze the question.

The response was instant.

Not yet.

"What does that mean?" Allison asked. "The women aren't there? Was George at a secondary location when Blaze found him? Or does it mean there's someone higher on the food chain than George? Someone scarier? Did Blaze ask Redmon about George?"

Thunder rolled, and lightning flashed. Derek shook his head again. The predicted storm was going to show its face after all. Three storms in three nights. With any luck, there wouldn't be any severe flooding to divide manpower at the police department or any wind damage, like downed trees and power lines, to stop Blaze and his team from recovering the women. Wherever they were.

Derek stood, squashing the urge to pace. He didn't have the answers she wanted, and it wasn't the time to interrupt his brothers with more questions. "How do you feel about making s'mores while we wait for our next update?"

Allison slouched against her seat, then frowned. She glanced outside, where the sky had grown dark with storm clouds, and trees whipped in the growing wind. "I'm not sure this is the right weather for that."

Derek pointed into the living room. "We have a fireplace."

A sweet smile bloomed on her lips, and she laughed. "Why not? I could definitely use the distraction right now, and I haven't had s'mores since I was a little girl."

"Time to change that," he said. "I'll get the ingredients. You grab a blanket and pillows for us to sit on."

"Deal."

Derek hit the light switch on the wall as he made his way back to her, and the room was cast in radiant streaks of red and purple as storm clouds battled the sunset outside the windows.

He sat closely to Allison as they held their marshmallows on pokers over the fire, then assembled their evening sweets.

Rain slid over the windows and danced on the roof, coming faster and harder at times, more easily and rhythmically at others.

"How can this moment be so perfect," Allison whispered, "and still be part of something so awful?"

"You think this is perfect?" Derek asked, smiling as he sucked a dollop of gooey marshmallow off his fingertip.

She laughed. "How lame am I, right?"

"I think you're pretty amazing, actually," he said, instantly caught in her hopeful gaze.

"You do?"

He frowned. Did she really not know? "Yes."

"And I'm not a terrible person for being so happy right now?"

Derek felt his eyebrows pull deeper. "Of course not. You've got to find the good in life and grab on to it wherever you can, because bad stuff is happening everywhere. All the time. If you get so hung up on that you miss everything else, what was the point?"

Allison's concerned expression bled into surprise, then something far more intense. Her gaze dropped to his mouth, and he fought the urge to pull her against him.

"Allison," he whispered, holding his ground as she set aside her s'mores and worked her way onto her knees, coming closer, until he had to tip his head back to watch her.

She set her palms on his unshaven cheeks and stared intently into his eyes. "Is this okay?"

He grinned. Was she asking his permission to touch him? Did she imagine there was a world where he'd say no? "Only if you're going to kiss me soon. I'm getting all sorts of ideas down here."

Allison smiled, then lowered her lips to his, and he was gone for her.

Just like that.

No coming back.

And he didn't even care.

Chapter Twenty

Allison kissed Derek tentatively at first, testing the boundaries and desperate not to cross a line. It had taken her all day to get up the nerve to try. She'd been sure she felt their connection growing every minute, electric and intense, but she'd had so many other emotions to contend with. She couldn't be quite sure. Then each time she thought he might kiss her, he'd change the subject or walk away.

There was only one thing left to do, and that was test her theory.

So, she had. And it was marvelous.

The coarse stubble of his cheeks scratched against her palms, igniting little fires all over her skin as she imagined what it would feel like to have those cheeks grazing a path across her breasts, down her stomach and between her thighs.

She gasped at the imagery, and Derek moaned against her mouth in response. She drew her lips open as he slid his tongue inside.

Heat spread through her as she explored his tightly muscled chest, arms and back. She tugged the hem of his shirt from his jeans so she could feel the warmth and contours of his skin against her palms without hindrance or limitation.

He froze when her fingers found his abdomen and pulled back to search her eyes. "We don't have to rush," he said. "We don't have to do anything."

She could see the turmoil on his face. Caught between what he obviously wanted, if his physical response was any indication, and what he thought was right. She supposed he might imagine he wasn't being very chivalrous at the moment, but she wasn't looking for a white knight right now. All she wanted was Derek's body against hers, his lips on her mouth, his hands in her hair. And some time to ride the high of knowing Derek Winchester wanted her, too.

Allison stretched a thigh across his lap and lowered herself onto him, with his massive palms guiding her at her waist. Each of his touches were languid and unrushed, passionate without the pressure to do anything more than they were right now. And for the first time in her life, Allison felt cherished.

They kissed until her head spun and she panted to catch her breath. Then Derek drew her to him and laid her back against their blanket on the floor. He stretched out beside her and brushed hair from her cheeks, tucking it gently behind her ear. He looked at her as if she was the prize everyone wanted, but only he got to keep.

She hoped he would want to keep her, because the longer they spent together, the more certain she was that her heart would break when he left.

"Everything okay?" he asked, brushing his nose across her cheek.

"I was just thinking I've never been kissed like that before, and I like it."

Derek pressed his lips against her closed eyelids, then another to her temple, careful not to touch her bruised forehead. "You should be kissed like this every day and as much as you want."

"Got some vacation time coming?" she teased, opening her eyes and tracing the tip of her finger along his jaw.

"To spend kissing you?" he asked, eyebrows tented. "Let my boss try to stop me."

She laughed, then snuggled in close to his chest.

"I'd planned to wait until you were out of danger before making my move," he said. "Then I was going to stop by your place and invite you and Bonnie out for ice cream."

Her heart rate sped, and her barely cooling body flooded with fresh waves of pleasure. "You were going to ask me out? With Bonnie? And ice cream was your move?"

"I'd still like to. And Bonnie's a little young for whiskey, which is my only other move."

Allison smiled. "I never thought I'd find someone to care about after Bonnie was born. Not for eighteen years or so, at least. And here you are. A man I trust with my daughter. And someone I trust with our lives," she added. "Who popped up out of nowhere and kisses me until I'm dizzy then invites me out for ice cream."

"Anyone who wouldn't give you whatever you wanted isn't worth your time," Derek said. His low, gravelly voice spread goose bumps over her skin. He dipped his head and pressed wet kisses down the column of her throat and across her collarbone, only looking up when the thunder rolled, and Bonnie's responding complaint came down the hall and across the monitor.

Lightning illuminated the world outside the windows—a world that had gone black since she'd last bothered to take notice.

His phone buzzed, and he rose onto an elbow to pull it from his pocket and check the message.

"What does it say?" Allison asked, sitting up, attention divided between his text and Bonnie's quiet fusses.

"Blaze is holding George overnight for questioning," Derek said. "He lawyered up."

"So he's guilty?" she asked. Why else would he ask for an attorney?

"Maybe," Derek answered. "Career criminals like George know to always ask for a lawyer. With a record like his, things could go very poorly otherwise."

"But he's in custody overnight, so we can finally breathe?" she asked.

"I think we're safe as long as George is the guy Redmon was afraid of," he said, seeming to leave out something.

Allison considered that statement for a moment, then closed her eyes and dropped her face into waiting palms. "Blaze could have two criminals in custody for these crimes, and I'm still in danger."

"Better safe than sorry," Derek said. "So how about we wait for more details? Meanwhile, we'll be quiet, and pretend we aren't home."

She raised teasing eyes to his. "I'm not sure I can be quiet."

Derek groaned. He grabbed her wrists and pulled them around his neck. "You're killing me, Hill."

"Sorry," she whispered, not meaning it at all.

"Don't worry about it. I'm making big plans to die slowly."

They kissed the time away as the storm tried to take the cabin down around them, exploring boundaries and reveling in the sweet moments until a clap of thunder jarred the cabin and the power went out.

Bonnie cried. Not a drifting-back-to-sleep kind of cry, but one that indicated she was fully awake and needed her mama.

Allison kissed Derek once more, then wiggled out from beneath him. "Time for her nightly bottle with Mommy. Then maybe you and I can finish our argument from earlier about the sleeping arrangements."

Derek collapsed onto his back with a moan that said he wouldn't be putting up much of a fight when she returned.

She pushed to her feet, then mixed a bottle by the light of her phone's flashlight app.

The phone buzzed and vibrated with a severe weather announcement. Flash flood warnings for their county.

Thankfully, she, Bonnie and Derek were on a mountain.

Outside, the car alarm on Cruz's Jeep burst to life, and the headlights began to flash.

Allison froze, her baby's bottle in her hand. "Derek?"

"On it," he said, already moving toward the door. "Stay with Bonnie. I'll check it out." He grabbed his gun on the way through the door, and Allison hurried down the short hall to her baby.

A flash of lightning illuminated the room as she entered, and a woman glared at her from just inside the open window. She was wearing a black motorcycle jacket, boots and jeans. Her long black hair stuck to her neck and clothes in sopping tendrils.

She pressed one finger to her lips, then pointed a gun at the crib.

Chapter Twenty-One

Derek swiped Cruz's keys off the counter and grabbed his gun just in case. The porch light was out, thanks to the storm that had taken their electricity. He pointed the fob at the Jeep to stop the alarm, hoping Bonnie hadn't been too upset by the outburst. Frankly, he'd like to help get her back to sleep, then pick up with Allison where they'd left off.

The Jeep silenced at the press of the button.

Derek held perfectly still, listening to the forest around him. To the angry, rumbling storm and to the mostly silent cabin at his back.

Bonnie's cries wafted softly through the door, barely audible over the thunder and pelting rain.

He dialed Cruz as he made his way back inside. "The power's out here," he said by way of greeting. "The alarm on your Jeep was going off for no reason. Could the thunder have caused it?"

"I doubt it," Cruz said, sounding alert but a little confused. "Maybe the wind knocked a branch onto it."

Derek eyeballed the swaying trees. That was a likely possibility. "I'll let you know tomorrow."

"Why don't I just check it out myself? I'm only ten minutes out."

"From where?" Derek turned to stare down the mud-slicked road they'd driven in on.

"From you. I'm on my way to keep you company. I decided it would be best if I take a watch shift through the night," he said. "You took a heavy beating this morning, and you probably haven't slept since we lost Mason. Plus the storm could cause you all sorts of problems in an old cabin surrounded by trees. And, frankly, this case is giving me a rash. I'm here. I'm parking along the road and walking up. Then if the Jeep's stuck and you need to leave, there's an option on the main road."

"What do you mean this case is giving you a rash?" Derek said, repeating the statement back to him. "What's bugging you about it?"

"Everything," Cruz said, after a long pause. "Your brothers think I'm overreacting, but I don't overreact. Blaze is feeling confident, having George in custody, but we don't even know if this is our guy. What if he's involved, but he's not the one calling the shots? Or maybe he isn't involved at all. We could be chasing our tails while the women are being moved out of reach. I just don't like it. Too many ifs and unanswered questions."

Derek hated to say it, but he'd been thinking all the same things, and George wasn't the man he'd fought with earlier. So there was still at least one unnamed man directly involved in this. Whereabouts unknown.

"And I don't like this George guy deciding he wants to wait until he can get a lawyer in there before anyone else talks to him…that just rubs me the wrong way," Cruz continued. "I know this isn't his first time being hauled in for questioning, but he doesn't look the type to sit there quietly. He looks like the type who'd put up a fight, demand that it was unlawful detainment, even if he knew he was guilty. I told Blaze I didn't trust it. I think George is buying time."

"For what?" Derek asked, his heart rate picking up with each of Bonnie's cries.

"Who knows," Cruz said, "but whatever he's up to, you know it's no good."

The hairs on Derek's arms and along the back of his neck rose to attention. "Hang on," he said, tuning in to Bonnie's cries as they grew more fervent. He swore, knowing without seeing that he'd been distracted and duped once again. His gut clenched and twisted as he sprinted the short handful of steps down the hall to the closed bedroom door, then freed his sidearm and took shelter behind the wall. "Allison," he called, projecting his voice against the rolling thunder.

As expected, no one answered, and Bonnie continued to cry.

"What's going on?" Cruz demanded, his voice coming small and angry through the phone's speaker. Wind whipped and whistled over the line.

On a mental count of three, Derek kicked the door open and blinked against the darkness.

Rain streamed through an open window at the back of the room, sheer curtains billowing and dancing in the night.

While Bonnie screamed for her mother.

THREE HOURS LATER, Derek sat in the West Liberty PD conference room with his brothers and his partner, mentally thanking his parents for stepping in to care for Bonnie. Police from the department local to the cabin were scouring the woods in the rain for a lead on where Allison had gone, but the storm was making their progress nearly impossible. The rain masked Allison's scent from the K9s, and likely washed any potential evidence over the hill in tiny mudslides. Whatever the recovery units were still trying to do wouldn't last much longer, when lightning put an end to that, as well.

"So what do we know?" Blaze asked for the tenth time as Lucas made notes on a rolling whiteboard.

Derek's insides twisted until he thought he'd be sick. Allison was gone. Taken on his watch. Another partner lost.

"We know George is the kind of offender who'd have his hands all over a trafficking ring, if we're right about what this is," Lucas said. "We know one of the ATVs used in the most recent attack at Mason's place was titled to Lonnie Voss, a former girlfriend of George's. We know Redmon is the one who attacked Allison three times, at three locations, and voiced his orders to return her to someone who scares him." He moved his dry-erase marker from photograph to photograph, pointing out the key players known to them so far.

Allison's photo stood in the row of missing-person flyers.

Derek swallowed a mouthful of bile.

He stared at the whiteboard with its scribbles and lines and pictures. There were images of George, Redmon and Lonnie Voss, along with photos of the ATV from the river, and the crime scenes at both Allison and Mason's houses. He was missing a key piece of information, maybe more than one, but he had to work with what was in front of him. And he needed the details to amount to something big and fast before the raging storm let up. It was the only thing potentially slowing down the criminals. "How about the notations on the scrap of paper?" he asked. "You said you have an idea about dates and times. If the old mile markers give you locations. Where are they going next?"

Lucas moved closer to the enlarged photo of the paper that was now in evidence. "As far as we can tell, they've got another stop at sunrise, but the first part of the numbers change, and I can't tell where that'll be."

Blaze crept closer to the board, studying the map. "I'll contact the counties south of us, following the river. See if any of them have an outdated mile-marking system like we have. Maybe that will help put the location into focus."

"Good idea," Derek said. "Do you think they'll leave with two key players in custody?"

Cruz tapped his thumbs against the table's edge. "They'll leave if the guys we have are low on the totem pole. If they aren't, they could still have a contingency plan."

"The boss could be the grunt I knocked out in the river," Derek said.

"Agreed. We need to get an identity on him ASAP," Blaze said. "Maybe you can take another look at the database."

"Yeah." Derek suppressed a growing roar. There wasn't time to look at thousands of faces in search of one that might not even be there, but he had to do whatever her could. Allison was in danger. Scared and alone. And Bonnie would be an orphan if he didn't get her mother back safely.

He thought again of his parents' willingness to care for Bonnie while he helped his brothers search for Allison. It broke his heart that the Hills didn't have a family like his to lift them up. Maybe one day, if he played his cards right, Allison would consider sharing his family and his last name.

All of that hinged on what happened next.

Blaze crossed his arms. "I'll get you set up with the database when we finish here." He looked back to the board. "Redmon still isn't talking. He knows we can't tie him to Mason's murder, only confirm his presence after the fact. And as far as the murder, there's no weapon or witness, since a punch to the chest, plus emotional distress, was probably what stopped Mason's heart. We don't know who hit him. Redmon will be charged with a bag of smaller crimes. Things he's done to Allison, breaking and entering, stalking and attempted abduction. But if we charge him on those things, he'll be out in no time. If we tie him to the human trafficking, and find this missing woman who was present at the murder, all changes for Redmon."

Derek leaned forward, elbows on knees, willing the whiteboard to speak to him. "How'd he react when you mentioned George? Doesn't seem like he'd be in a hurry to go to jail with someone he's so afraid of."

Blaze shifted, his eyes narrowed. "He didn't respond when I asked him the same thing."

That didn't go along with the picture Allison had painted. "So Redmon tells Allison he'd rather go to jail than show up without her, wherever his boss was. But he wouldn't mind going to prison with the guy?" Derek cussed, as the words fell from his tongue. "Because it's not a guy," he said, stepping forward, eyes glued to the whiteboard.

The smaller set of boot prints left at Mason's house the night he died. The strand of long black hair on his flannel.

Derek was willing to bet the one person they'd completely overlooked in all of this had size eight boots and DNA to match that long black hair found on Mason. "Lonnie Voss has been pulling the strings all along."

Chapter Twenty-Two

Allison woke to the acrid smells of stale air, urine and body odor. The world rocked around her, and somewhere distant, the storm raged. Her stomach revolted and she pried open her eyes. She rolled onto her side and gave up the s'mores and tea. Her insides cramped and ached in their absence.

She batted her eyes as foggy memories returned, and the haze of the moment began to fade away. There was only a narrow strip of light to see by, perhaps streaming in from beneath a closed door. Her head pounded as she forced herself back to full consciousness, instinct clawing at her limbs to move. The constant ebbing motion kept her still. Seasickness pressed her to the floor, and she begged the cool damp boards to pull the heat from her cheek and stave off the blinding nausea.

Allison was definitely on a boat.

"I think she's awake," someone whispered.

Allison dragged her eyes open once more. Panic tightened her core. She couldn't run. Couldn't fight.

A collection of muddled voices echoed around her, soft white noise against the backdrop of the storm.

She shivered and realized she was curled into a fetal position, wearing clothing drenched through with mud and rain. The fuzzy memories began to firm, and she recalled walking obediently off the mountain in a deluge, often sliding and rolling farther than the single step she'd taken had intended.

Allison had been held at gunpoint by a woman who'd pointed the weapon at her baby.

There had been a detached, single-minded look in the woman's eyes when she told Allison to climb out the window, and it had struck terror into Allison's marrow.

The woman had threatened and cursed as they'd made the long, dangerous trek down the mountain. She blamed Allison for getting the authorities involved in Mason's murder. And for her part in landing two of her lackeys in jail. She'd said she was on a schedule and Allison was slowing her down. That time was money, and now Allison was going to work off any losses she'd caused. The woman had sneered as she stuffed her into a waiting truck on a towpath halfway to the main road. She'd told Allison that life as she knew it had officially ended. She would soon be a heroin addict. The sale and use of her body would be frequent and to any bidder.

Allison had asked whom she was being sold to before the woman had injected her with something that numbed her thoughts and limbs. The woman had answered with a resigned, almost remorseful tone.

Allison wasn't being sold to a person. She was being added to a mobile collection of women who entertained at parties. They were handed to the guests like gift bags or door prizes for attending. And that, the woman had told her, was why she'd be thankful for the heroin.

Allison groaned, stomach churning and head screaming. She didn't know how long she'd been unconscious, but every minute she stayed on the boat equated to her being moved farther from home. From the people who were surely looking for her. And from her baby.

Forcing herself to roll toward the quiet commotion, she squinted at the myriad of shadows. *People*, she realized, crouched and huddling in the hot, confined space. These were the missing women she'd been trying to find and save, and she'd become one of them.

The angelic face of an emaciated young woman came slowly into view.

A spark of recognition kindled in Allison's addled mind. "Cari?"

The whispering stirred up again.

"You know me?" the woman asked, hope and distrust fighting in her wary eyes.

"Yes," Allison answered, her thick, dry tongue sticking to the roof of her mouth.

Cari was the one who'd made it off the boat. She'd risked everything to save these women. Cari was an ally.

"We have to get off this boat."

Fat tears fell from Cari's eyes. "We can't."

"We can," Allison said. "You have. I know."

A small sob broke from Cari's lips. "I tried, and they were punished."

The other figures scooted forward, embracing Cari and shushing her. Some in comfort. Some in warning. Several of these women had been badly beaten. Bruises darkened their cheeks and arms.

"If we try to leave," Cari said, "they hurt the others."

A new heaviness settled on Allison's shoulders, and her insides seemed to hollow. This was how the captors kept them all in line. One woman's misstep meant pain for all the others. "We have to try again," Allison said, careful to keep her voice low. "I know you made it once, and this time you won't be alone."

Cari stared, lips trembling.

The battered figures around her shook their heads, not wanting to receive their captor's wrath again.

"Please," Allison begged. "These men killed my friend, the man who tried to help you."

Cari covered her mouth to stifle the sounds of body-shaking sobs that followed. A filthy, tattered bandage sat on her forearm, possibly evidence of Mason's help.

"His name was Mason Montgomery, and I wasn't his only friend." Allison told the group her story. About the Winchesters. The police department that had been searching for them, and about finding the paper with clues to their schedule.

Cari's sobs grew soft. "That's what was on the paper?" She wiped her eyes, a strained smile growing. "I didn't know. Only that all the guards have one, and they guarded it with their lives. I took Redmon's from his pocket when he took me into the woods to…" She paused, then averted her eyes. "I got away afterward, when he had to let me go to fasten his pants. I ran, and I hid until night. Then I saw a light at a home, and I went toward it. I fell while making my way along the riverbank, and gashed my arm on something sharp. I tried to stop the bleeding with my sweater, but it soaked through. When I got to the house, the old man helped me. He cleaned and bandaged the wound. Then they found me."

So, it had been Cari's blood on Mason's shirt.

"You did great," Allison said. "If you hadn't done that, I wouldn't be here, and all those cops wouldn't be looking for us."

Cari began to cry again. "But that man is dead because of me."

"And he'd give his life again," Allison said, choking on the weight and truth of the words, "if he knew it would save just one of you. We have a chance to save us all. But we have to get out at the next stop," she said. "The police will be there looking for us, but we'll have to let them know we're there. If we work together, we can overtake the woman and the guards. We can cause a commotion to draw attention to this boat. We can win. And we can go home."

"No. We can't," a small, quaking voice said from the back of the huddle. "I've been here a long time. It's worse for us if we fight."

"Well, I want to try." A young woman with a determined expression inched closer to Allison. She was cleaner than the others, and her clothes still smelled of perfume.

Allison recognized her immediately from the missing-person flyers. She was the high-school senior who'd just been taken from a shopping center in West Liberty. "Thank you, Zoey."

"You know me, too?" she asked, hope rising in her voice.

"I know all of you. Or most of you, I think. I've been working with the police since my friend was killed and we figured out Cari had been there and why." She scanned their stunned and cautious faces, some bruised and filthy. Others with the vacant stares of women who'd been gone too long and would never fully return, not even when this was years behind them. She swallowed tears and forced assurance into her voice. "The police are looking for all of you. They've connected Bailey, Cari, Zoey, Genny, Hannah, Lexi and Meg. They are coming," she promised. "We have to help them find us."

"It's worse if we fight," the frightened woman repeated, this time with sincere terror.

"It's not worse," Zoey said. "Death wouldn't be worse than this."

"This *is* death," Cari said, emphasizing the middle word. "You can't understand what comes next, and you don't want to. Because when it does…" She trailed off a moment, then straightened, chin jutting out. "You'll wish you were dead."

Many of the others looked away, eyes downcast,

profound and painful understanding carved on their gaunt faces.

"They know," Allison said softly, reaching for Cari's hand.

"Then they need to fight," she stressed, voice rising in indignation.

The others leaped at her with shushes and whispers.

Cari pushed them away, mouth closed and expression hard. Maybe feeling guilty for her outburst.

Allison added guilt and shame to the list of tools their captors used to control them.

"We can do this," Allison insisted. "You aren't alone."

The words lodged in her throat, solid and filled with truth. These women weren't alone anymore, and neither was she.

Chapter Twenty-Three

Lonnie's home was overrun with police officers by the time Derek and his brothers arrived. The woman of interest was long gone, along with the black Ford pickup registered in her name, but a conscientious judge had granted a search warrant. And for that, Derek was eternally grateful.

Blaze and Lucas made numerous phone calls before leaving the police station, alerting law enforcement, as well as the coast guard and park rangers, to the situation. No one was sure where the abducted women were now, but they suspected the mode of transport was a boat.

Everyone with any kind of authority worked to match the numbers from the scrap of paper found at Mason's house to a location within their jurisdiction.

And the Winchesters were digging in however they could. Starting with Lonnie's home in Marsh County.

Derek followed Blaze and Lucas through the crowd of onlookers, drawn to the lights and chaos on a dark and stormy night. People raised cell phones to capture the scene. They wondered aloud what had happened, and if the homeowner was okay. Derek lingered on the stumpy postage-stamp yard, rain sheeting over his face and jacket as he listened as uniformed officers questioned the crowd.

According to neighbors clutching raincoats and wrestling umbrellas against the wind, Lonnie was a private person with plenty of visitors, but she'd never developed relationships with the people on her street. She came and went quietly, and there was always a different car in her drive.

They recognized photos of George when asked. He'd been too angry and tattooed to miss as he came and went in a truck that needed a muffler.

But no one had a clue about Lonnie's current location. No one knew where she went when she left home. They had no ideas about her personal interests or hangouts.

Because no one on this street knew her at all.

"Derek," Lucas called, turning him toward the home's front porch. "Come on," he urged, waving from the open front door.

He moved immediately in his brother's direction, desperate for whatever scrap of hope he would offer.

Lonnie's small lawn and flowerbeds were tidy, if currently a little flooded. The planters and welcome mat at her door were warm and inviting. Not a single clue to indicate the property's owner was a sick and twisted criminal. A woman who struck fear in the hearts of derelicts, and used them to abduct and sell other women.

Tension worked in Derek's muscles, tightening them to the point of pain. His jaw, neck and shoulders screamed with every hurried movement. He hadn't relaxed in hours, maybe not days.

"There's a white BMW in the garage," Lucas said. "Heavy tint on the windows. Plates are registered to an LLC in Louisville. No signs of the pickup."

Derek stuck close as Lucas skirted around the peppering of officers, taking photos and searching every cabinet, box and laundry basket. "Lonnie owns an LLC?" Derek asked, taking in the scene and the new information as they moved.

She'd been arrested for fraud and passing bad checks. He supposed she could've used the LLC for money laundering, or maybe buying and selling women was her main business these days.

Lucas stopped inside a first-floor bedroom. "The closet's filled with typical middle-class biker attire. Jeans. T-shirts. Leather vests. Motorcycle boots. And lots of them. But…" He approached the open closet and shoved the hangers to one side, revealing another style of clothing. "She also has some nice pantsuits with jackets, blouses, heels, the whole nine yards."

"What's a biker need with all that corporate casual?" Derek asked, approaching the closet.

Lucas pulled a pair of gloves from his pocket and passed them to his brother. "Or a white BMW."

Derek snapped the protection over his hands, then thumbed through the items in question. His mind raced back to the whiteboard at the police station. "It's a cover," he said, the pieces beginning to filter into place. "We've been assuming the missing women were attacked and dragged off by the goons who kept coming for Allison, but what if a nicely dressed woman in her late thirties and driving a BMW approached them?" The idea took shape as he spoke the words. "Women trust women, right? Maybe she pretended she needed help with something? The dark tint would hide whatever was going on as she took them away."

Lucas rubbed his chin in consideration. "That would work. I wonder how she convinced them all to go with her."

Derek pulled a fancy leather purse from a shelf above the hangers and checked the interior pockets. He followed suit with the next two bags. "She only had to get the women close enough to force them inside. Maybe by gun or at knifepoint." His fingertip collided with the edge of something at the bottom of the purse in hand. He fished it out and stared.

"What do you have?" Lucas asked, moving in for a closer look.

"A business card for Sophia Lions, a talent scout with Top Model Management." He turned the card to face Lucas, nausea pooling in his core.

Lonnie Voss's photo was printed on the bottom corner. She wore a huge smile and a white suit jacket like the one in her closet.

"Hey." Blaze's voice jerked the pair to attention. "What's that?"

Derek passed him the business card, and Blaze's mouth turned down. "Well, that answers how these women were taken in broad daylight and no one noticed them making a scene, or even remembered seeing anything out of the ordinary." He slid the card into an evidence bag. "A lot of the victims were young, maybe still naive enough to suspend any suspicions they might've had in favor of hope." He sighed. "Well, we can reach out to the locations where women went missing and search parking-lot security feeds for the BMW. I assume this—" he shook the baggie with the business card "—explains why she has that in her garage. Can't exactly pretend to be a model scout while driving an old Ford."

Derek nodded. "You having any luck out there?"

Blaze looked over his shoulder, toward the rest of the house. "Yeah. Tech has something I want you guys to look at."

Derek followed Blaze back through the home with Lucas on his heels.

"There are some photographs of the river, bridges and beaches on a laptop," Blaze said. "The files names are all numbers. I'm hoping those numbers will match up with others from the paper. I also thought we might recognize something from one of Dad's excursions."

Derek picked up his pace as the dining room came into view.

A woman in a navy blue windbreaker was seated at the table, working gloved fingers over a laptop's keyboard. She looked up as the men approached.

Blaze extended an arm in his brothers' direction. "Lucas and Derek Winchester. Lucas is a West Liberty SVU Detective. Derek runs a local PI firm and had been offering Ms. Hill and her daughter protection for several days. Until Ms. Hill's disappearance tonight."

The woman looked from Lucas to Derek. "I'm Nina Chase, Marsh County Sheriff's Department. Feel free to pull up a chair." She turned back to the screen and enlarged a number of photos, then began to flip through the images using the touch pad. "Most of the files on this device had been deleted. It was the cleanest machine I'd ever seen at first glance. Nothing unusual. Shopping. News. Weather. But the trash had been dumped, and people just don't do that. They think putting it in the bin means it's gone. Even those who understand how it works don't do it often enough. Once I have more time with this in the lab, I'm sure I'll get most of the files back. Meanwhile, I accessed her history, which she didn't erase, and logged in to her email, where I found a number of messages from the same account, often with attachments. These are the attachments."

Derek dragged a chair to her side, as she'd suggested. His brothers huddled behind.

"Recognize anything?" she asked, moving through the images like a slideshow.

"Not yet," Derek said. "Keep going."

Photos of overgrown fields and rocky shores flipped past, followed by long-forgotten homes, dilapidated barns and broken-down signs advertising local produce, goods or service. Finally, a rusted-out tractor older than their grandfather.

All the images felt vaguely familiar, in fuzzy, mostly forgotten ways. Childhood memories that had faded to near extinction, but wiggled loosely at the photos.

Derek had traveled the river with his dad and brothers many times, and for many miles, as a kid, but the scenery was never a big draw. He'd been more interested in the snacks their mother had packed, swimming along beside the canoe in the rushing tepid water and tormenting his little brothers at every possible turn.

"Wait." Derek pointed at the laptop. "Go back."

The image changed again, and a grove of trees in full bloom was centered the screen. Memories of the sweetened air rushed over him as if the moment was happening now. "That's an apple orchard." He turned to Blaze and Lucas. "The old tractor wasn't far from there. I remember it now."

His brothers stared, likely searching their own minds for this memory. They were one and two years younger than Derek, so it was possible they wouldn't recall, but Derek did. Vividly now, and more so with each passing second.

Blaze barked a sudden and unexpected laugh. "We hit each other with crab apples that rolled over the banks into the river."

Nina brought up another photo. "Like these?"

"Yeah," Derek answered. An image of a faded and hole-filled dinghy anchored the image, but behind it, a gnarled and reaching tree hung heavy with crab apples.

"But those trees won't have fruit for a while," Derek said. "I'm not even sure they're in bloom yet."

"Doesn't matter," Nina said. "These photos were likely taken as surveillance, while the routes and stops were being selected and planned. The dates on the emails span more than a year."

Derek nodded in somber understanding. This wasn't something Lonnie and her crew had rushed into with crossed fingers and a prayer. This was designed with patience and executed with precision. "They've outsmarted us from the start."

"Until now," Blaze said. "We've finally got a new lead, and we're running with it."

Nina went back to the photos, making notes of the familiar ones and their file names. The photo taken near Mason's river access was named with the letters and number on the marker by the water. "I'm not sure what the pattern is here, or the relevance. There aren't any busy shopping areas for miles from this orchard or your friend's home."

Blaze pressed his hands to the back of Derek's chair, leaning closer for a better look. "Maybe it's a map for the route. Visual cues to keep them on track?"

"Maybe," Nina responded. "I'll send the files to the coast guard and park rangers. Maybe they can fill in the locations of images you don't recognize. Meanwhile we can try to match the photo names you know with numbers from your paper."

Derek looked at his watch, shocked by the amount of time that had passed, and how little was left before the next stop would be made. They needed to hustle if they planned to identify, then reach, the location in time to save Allison and the others. And the new thread of hope had quickly run thin.

Nina pushed away from the table. "I need to return some phone calls, and I want to follow up on the files sent, make sure everyone is aware of the time sensitivity here. Let me know if you see anything else that strikes a memory."

Derek dragged the laptop into reach and began to move the photos around, putting them in geographical order, as he remembered seeing them on those long trips.

"What are you doing?" Blaze asked. "Reordering by file name or location on the river?"

"Location," Derek said. "I'm trying to create a big picture. See if we can knock loose some kind of pattern."

"Hey, Winchesters," Nina called. "Coast Guard's got something that might match up with your numbers."

She turned her phone screen, revealing the image of a mile marker along a stretch of river Derek didn't recognize.

"Where is that?" he asked.

"Rex Bend."

Hope warred with panic in Derek's chest. Rex Bend was nearly to Tennessee by way of the river, but it was still in Kentucky. "How far is that by highway?" he asked, pushing onto his feet and moving backward toward the front door.

"About a hundred miles," Nina answered, "but it's a busy port. We'll need to get a more exact location if we want to set up a sting."

Adrenaline roared, hot and heavy, through Derek's blood. He felt as if he might be able to run there more quickly than his brother could drive.

"We're leaving now," Blaze told Nina. "Text the location when you have it."

"It's almost five thirty," Derek said, jogging back across the flooded lawn toward Blaze's truck. A sting would need to be in place before Lonnie and her lackeys arrived with the women, or law enforcement would lose the advantage. "Next stop is at seven," he said, swinging into the passenger side while Lucas climbed into the extended cab's back seat. "A hundred miles in ninety minutes. It's going to be close, even by highway. And sooner would be better."

Blaze set the destination on his dashboard GPS, then slid the shifter into Drive. "Then we'd better get moving."

Chapter Twenty-Four

Allison and her makeshift army sat against the wall farthest from the door, attention fixed on the narrow band of light bleeding beneath. She'd helped move the handful of clearly drugged women to another wall during the night, leaving an unobstructed path to the door for those who would fight.

The ultimate goal was to get at least one woman off the boat. Whoever managed to escape would bring attention to their plight and alert authorities. Hopefully, help would already be there. Waiting and watching for signs of the captives' location.

Only one woman, Lisa, was awake, but she was unable to help with their plan. She'd been a naysayer from the start, controlled and immobilized by fear. So Lisa would lie with the unconscious women and pretend to be like them. Anything to avoid Lonnie's wrath in the event this coup failed. Allison didn't blame Lisa for her decision. How could she fault any of these women for whatever they did to survive?

Sounds of life slowly began to filter through the floorboards and hull. The bleat of a tugboat. The footfalls of their captors. The scent of fresh black coffee.

Allison didn't know where they were, or which way to run if she made it off the boat, but she knew dawn meant they would dock soon. At least, that was how Blaze had interpreted the notations on the paper Cari dropped outside Mason's home. She hoped more than anything that he was right, and that the Winchesters had figured out where the boat was stopping. Because if they didn't know where to find her, then Allison was on her own.

Doubts crept into her mind, replacing the bravado that had inflated throughout the night.

What if Allison made it off the boat, but the port wasn't busy? What if there weren't any witnesses to ask for help? What if she was recaptured and dragged back? Or worse, killed on the spot? The remaining women would be punished for her failure. Lonnie and her crew would vanish with their captives, and without a trace.

"I think we're slowing down," Cari whispered. "They'll bring us water and something to eat soon. They always come in twos. One will deliver the meals, then check the pulses on them." She cast a sad look at the motionless bodies curled on the floor. "The second guy will have a knife or weapon of some sort to keep us still and quiet while the first does his work."

"Not a gun?" Allison asked, a flicker of hope rising once more. Redmon had always had a gun when he'd come for her.

"Not on the boat," Cari said, as if the suggestion was crazy. "It could put a hole in the hull."

"Oh, right." Taking on water was a poor idea anytime, but especially with eleven people trapped below deck. "A few gunshots would be great for getting some attention, though."

"Yeah," Zoey said dryly, from her position beside Cari. "Lonnie's attention."

"And good luck getting near enough to pull the trigger without being on the wrong side of the barrel," Cari said.

Allison shivered at the thought. She wished she knew how many men were upstairs with their leader. How many bigger, stronger, more nourished humans would she and her group have to fight? And how would Lonnie respond to the revolt? "Not well" seemed like a serious understatement. Allison had no doubt Lonnie would kill without hesitation.

The footfalls overhead grew louder as the boat continued to slow.

Lisa curled on the floor beside the four women who wouldn't wake.

Allison huddled in close with the five who were ready to fight. Cari and Zoey were most certain of their course. Bailey, Genny and Hannah less confident, but they were willing to try, and that was all Allison could ask.

The tumbler on the door's lock rolled, and tension ignited in the hull, momentarily extracting the oxygen from Allison's lungs and the small dark space.

"We need a distraction for the one who keeps

guard," Cari said. "The other guy will be focused on finding pulses once the food is distributed."

The group had already agreed to use their water bottles and breakfast trays as weapons.

Most importantly, they'd agreed to be as quiet as possible when they attacked, because six against two was almost a fair fight, and alerting more guards wouldn't help their cause.

Allison's army was physically weak and mentally drained, but their will to live was strong. And hope could move mountains.

The door opened, and a stream of blinding light flooded in, along with a fresh, sweet gust of cool air.

Allison squinted against the rays of sunrise, fiery red and eerily foreshadowing of the fight that was to come.

"Rise and shine," a lean, lanky man growled. His narrow frame and long limbs swung in jerky unsteady ways as the boat moved to another, lower gear. He sneered at the group, his cracked lips pulling back to reveal a tragic set of yellow-and-black teeth. A long black flashlight hung from his grip, metal and foreboding. A weapon in more ways than one. "Who wants breakfast?"

A second, stouter man followed the first into the hull, kicking the door shut behind him and sending them back into darkness. He was weighted with bags on each shoulder and began distributing food and water immediately, as Cari had promised. One sack was filled with bottles of water. Another contained a pile of small pie tins, which were handed out as trays, then a small orange, a bread roll and a hunk of cheese were delivered to each tray.

Allison traded looks with her team, all eyes still adjusting to the sudden change in light. Every set of fingers curled purposefully around their trays.

"Ah, ah, ah," the gangly man warned, raising the flashlight's beam into Allison's eyes, then blinding the others one by one. "Don't go getting any ideas. You're not here to think," he said. "If you need a reminder about why you're here, I'll be glad to give it to you."

The second man lowered himself to the floor, checking each woman for breath and a pulse.

Allison flinched when the beam of light returned to her. A long arm snaked out, curling fingers in Allison's hair.

He yanked her onto her feet and pressed her against him in a move that brought tears to her eyes. He tucked the flashlight under his opposite arm, its beam aimed at the group of horrified women. His filthy, calloused hand groped at Allison's body.

Her stomach rolled and her mind wept. The escape plan had been thwarted. All hope completely dashed in one single move by this thug. And the women hadn't even had the chance to take action.

The sound of a zipper pulled her thoughts back to the moment, and she realized the groping hand had moved onto unleashing his fly.

"No." A sob croaked out of her as she began to twist and fight. "Don't. Please."

"Keep begging," he said. "I like it. You need to

know I'm in charge. And you are nothing." His sour breath rolled across her face as he growled. The button on her jeans was unfastened with the tug of his fingers, and the zipper torn angrily down.

"Ken?" the other man said, a measure of fear in his tone. "Something's wrong with this one."

A strange thumping drew her attacker's attention to the collection of sleeping bodies.

"I'll be back for you," he said, throwing Allison to the ground at his feet.

She jerked up her zipper and fastened her button with shaking hands.

He pointed his flashlight at a woman who was apparently having severe convulsions. Ken swore, then took an awkward step toward the commotion.

Allison choked back another sob at the sight of Lisa's body flopping and pounding against the floorboards, spit rolling from her mouth.

The most frightened among them had found the strength to intercede, to prevent Allison's rape and to cause a perfect distraction.

"Hold her down," Ken snarled, kneeling at the other man's side, and setting his flashlight on the floor by his knee.

Together, the men pressed their palms to Lisa's legs and shoulders.

And Allison dove for the flashlight.

Chapter Twenty-Five

Derek stared over the river at Rex Bend, a public port at the edge of a thriving waterfront community. Cafés and shops lined the street, opposite the water. Early rising joggers were already out alongside dog walkers and commuters. He and his brothers had split up upon arrival, all awaiting details from Nina, the local coast guard, police or port authority on which vessel could be moving trafficked women.

Because even if Derek was in the right town, there were an unlimited number of places Allison could be. A fishing vessel? A yacht? Hidden in the hull? Packed into a cargo container? And how long did he have to find her before she would be gone again?

He bent and flexed his fingers at his sides, processing the nervous energy that pulsed through his veins. He paused at a bench to check his phone for possible missed messages, preferably ones announcing the recovery of Lonnie's vessel, with all the women safely inside. But there was nothing new.

In the distance, dawn crested the water like a fireball, spreading red fingers across the river and backlighting everything with its brilliant glow. Silhouettes of boats appeared in every shape and size, skating over the illuminated water. Many of the vessels were likely piloted by undercover authorities, searching, as Derek was, for that one unidentified craft.

"Come on," he coaxed the universe, whispering softly into the wind.

Allison believed things happened for reasons, often bigger than people could understand until much later. She thought there was some sort of sense to things, even the awful ones, and especially those that couldn't be explained. Derek had shrugged off the concept before, not subscribing to it, but hadn't been willing to ruin it for her, either.

Right now, he needed her belief to be true. He needed a sign.

Three distinct cracks broke the still morning air, and Derek's limbs tightened. There was no mistaking the sound of gunshots, and their presence at this river port, right now, could only mean one thing.

Wherever the sounds had come from, Allison wouldn't be far.

Derek broke into a run along the river, racing in the direction of the sounds. Several boats seemed to head that way, too.

Pedestrians stopped at the edge of the dock, staring toward a lone white fishing boat at the end. Dark nets draped over the sides, and the boat had begun to tilt.

Derek's lungs burned as he pushed himself harder and faster toward the apparently sinking vessel.

Men and women lined the rails of an approaching boat, their reflective jackets emblazoned with the logo of their official department. "Rex Bend Port Authority," a deep male voice called through a bullhorn. "Prepare to be boarded."

The fishing boat's motor churned to life, and the craft tilted precariously further.

Men in SWAT gear fell into step with Derek as he bolted down the long wooden dock.

A door on the fishing boat's cabin swung open, and his heart leaped in anticipation. A throng of bodies appeared on deck. They were screaming and swinging their arms overhead. The collection of women all crying out for help.

Allison wasn't among them.

ALLISON'S EYES OPENED as the rush of cold water touched her face. Sunlight streamed in from the open door to the boat's hull. Around her, five sleeping women were slowly becoming submerged in the climbing water. Everyone else was gone.

A thunderous voice boomed somewhere outside the open door. A bullhorn, perhaps. Maybe help was on its way.

She pulled herself into a seated position, and pain spread through her side. The accompanying memory caused her to cry out. She'd been shot, but so had Ken.

His slumped form leaned against the wall.

The second man had pulled a gun when Allison

struck Ken with his flashlight. Cari had lunged for the weapon, and the gun had gone off, taking Ken's life and making a hole in the hull. A second shot had pierced Allison's side. Lonnie had appeared in the doorway and taken the second man with her, cursing his ignorance for putting holes in the boat and killing her only other guard.

There were only two captors left, two obstacles between the captives and freedom, but Lonnie had locked the door and left them to drown.

Allison couldn't remember the rest, but the door was open now, and that was an excellent sign.

The rising water level around her was not.

"Wake up!" she screamed at the unconscious women, dragging herself to where they were lying in the tilted hull. "Wake up!"

A groan escaped the nearest body, and Allison collapsed beside her on the floor. "You've got to move, or you're going to die."

Tears rolled over Allison's cheeks, and the water pooled crimson around them. She was bleeding heavily, but she was conscious and she could still help the others.

She pulled one lifeless arm across her shoulders, then forced herself onto her knees, bearing her weight and that of the other woman as she dragged her to the short set of steps.

"ALLISON!" DEREK LEAPED onto the nearly capsized vessel as the officers hauled Lonnie and a man away in handcuffs.

"No!" A nearby woman yanked herself free from an officer's protective hold. "You have to help the others! There are more of us! They're drugged and one was shot!"

The other battered-looking women began to wrestle their saviors, too.

Derek's heart clenched with the selfish hope that Allison wasn't the one who'd been shot, knowing that would only mean that someone else had been. He dove toward the open door where the women seemed so desperate to go. And a pack of officers followed suit.

"They've got this," a familiar voice bellowed at his back. *Blaze*, Derek realized. His brother had made it. "Allison would want you to get the help you need," he told them. "Let these men and women help her now."

Derek stopped short at the flight of stairs. A pile of motionless bodies was stacked on the rungs below him, their arms and tattered clothing lifted by the rising water.

Beyond the steps, Allison held a woman to her chest, their faces haloed in crimson water.

And Allison's eyes slowly slid shut.

Chapter Twenty-Six

Allison opened her eyes to the bright lights of a hospital room, much like the one where she'd delivered Bonnie not too long ago. The scents of fresh flowers and stale coffee mixed with bleach and bandages hung in the air. "Bonnie," she croaked, pressing up, onto her elbows.

The room blurred and spun around her.

A quick beeping echoed the pace of her racing heart.

And Derek appeared with a strange woman in blue scrubs. His expression was solemn. Hers comforting. The woman fiddled with the IV bag hanging at her side, while Derek squeezed Allison's hand. "Not yet," he said. "You sleep for now. Bonnie will be here soon."

When Allison woke again, Derek was playing cards on her bed beside her legs. A crowd of people filled the space inside her little room.

"There's nothing wrong with doing it in a hospital," a woman said. "It doesn't matter where it happens, only that it happens."

"It doesn't seem very romantic," Derek said, apparently losing the round of cards to himself. He collected and shuffled them, eyes fixed on someone outside Allison's view. "I'm not trying to ambush her. Who invited all of you, anyway?"

"Well," an older woman said, "when you told me you were considering a proposal, I thought the family would want to know."

Allison pried her heavy lids open at that comment, then squinted at the group gathered around her. Was she hallucinating? Or did someone say Derek was planning a proposal? And wasn't there a limitation to the number of visitors an unconscious person could have?

"She's awake," someone whispered. And another memory returned with a resounding slap.

"The others," she whispered. "Cari, Zoey. Hannah, Genny." Her thick tongue stuck to the roof of her mouth as she spoke, but their names needed to be heard. "Bailey. Lisa."

"They're okay." Derek said, rising to his feet, then leaning over her. "All the other women are okay. Most are with their families, already evaluated and discharged. A few are staying for observation, but all will be okay now. Thanks to you." He smiled, then stroked hair away from her cheeks and forehead. "You can see them later, if you want." Concern pooled in his dark eyes, blending with compassion and something so much more. "How are you feeling?"

"Okay," she said, unsure if it was the truth or a lie. A fuzzy, warm sensation numbed and lightened her. She suspected that was a result of something put into her IV. "Bonnie?" she asked, sore eyes searching the room for signs of her baby.

"Here she is," the older woman's voice announced. A moment later, Derek's mom, Rosa, appeared with Bonnie dressed in a red-and-white plaid square-dancing costume, complete with red cowgirl boots and a ribbon for her baby's barely existent hair. "We've been taking great care of her. She's played with her cousins and all of us. Plus the animals. She loves to see the animals. And we went shopping." Rosa smiled. "I'm not sure she's ever been put down. We might've spoiled her a little."

Allison's eyes stung, and her already tight throat thickened. "Thank you."

Bonnie had not only avoided the tragedies of the boat, but she'd also had a wonderful time with people who made her smile and bought her frilly things.

Gratitude and love swelled in Allison's aching heart until she thought she wouldn't be able to breathe.

The crowd shifted and drew nearer, lining the sides of her bed as Rosa passed Bonnie into Allison's arms.

She snuggled her baby close and kissed her soft wispy hair. "I'm glad everyone is okay."

Blaze slung his arm around a redhead Allison didn't recognize. A little girl was nestled in the woman's arms. "Everyone's great except Ken," Blaze said. "He didn't make it. And his partners Mike and Lonnie aren't doing much better. They're going to jail, along with George and Redmon, where they will stay for a very long time. And thanks to George's willingness to spill every last detail he could think of, in exchange for leniency, more than twenty organizations across the country, known for throwing parties where trafficked women were delivered for entertainment, are being raided as we speak."

Relief and joy bloomed over her at the thought of all those events being busted, criminals being arrested and women saved. "When can I go home?"

A soft chuckle rolled over the room.

"Well, you were shot," Derek said. "You've been through a surgery to remove the bullet. Things went well, and you're recovering nicely, but you'll be here another day or two."

"Don't worry," Lucas said from his position near his parents and Gwen at the foot of her bed. "We'll all stop by every day."

The group laughed again, and this time Allison joined them.

"Oh, good," she said. "I won't be lonely."

"Not if I can help it," Derek said, heated eyes fixed on hers once more. "And I'm not sure how you'll feel about this, but your parents are on their way to see you. Cruz went to pick them up from the airport. You should probably get some more rest while you can."

Allison nodded, kissing Bonnie's head once more, then she passed her daughter into Derek's capable arms. "Protect her for me while I sleep."

"With my life," he said, cradling Bonnie against his chest. "Allison?"

"Yeah?" she asked, dragging her eyes back open, not realizing they'd already shut.

He leaned over the shiny silver bed rail once more and pressed a kiss to her forehead. "When you wake again, I have something I need to ask you."

Epilogue

Twelve months later

Allison pulled Derek to where she was sitting on the kitchen island, admiring his sexy frame in a stunning tuxedo. The home was dark and still around them, save for the snuffling of a sleeping old hound near the fire, and the occasional coo of their toddler through the monitor. These were some of her favorite moments. When the moon had risen, everyone was tucked safely into their beds or barns, and for a little while, the world contained only Allison and her very best friend.

"You taste like cake and champagne," she said, her sleek blue gown sliding up her thighs as she wrapped them around him.

"Are you sure?" He leaned in close, so she could kiss him again and check.

Blaze and Maisy had spared no expense on their wedding. A year of planning and countless helpers, and Allison didn't want to think about how many dollars had created a day no guest would soon forget. It was lavish and lovely with fancy things everywhere she'd looked.

Allison preferred the view before her. A man with whom she'd been through the unimaginable and back. One who still looked at her like she was the world's greatest prize. A prize he'd wisely claimed.

"You taste pretty good yourself," he said, offering her another bite of the chocolate-covered strawberries he'd swiped from Blaze and Maisy's dessert table on the way out.

Allison bit in greedily, eliciting a sigh from her beloved. "Since I won't be enjoying any champagne for the next six months or so, I figured I might as well indulge in whatever else I'd like."

Derek moaned again. "I like the sounds of that, Mrs. Winchester." He set a palm against her still flat stomach, and the usual storm brewed in his eyes. "Can you believe we're about to be parents again?"

"I can," she whispered, running a fingertip over his simple golden wedding band. "And I cannot wait."

Derek had legally adopted Bonnie the moment he and Allison were married, and he'd taken to fatherhood with the same pride and enthusiasm he extended to his role as her husband. She couldn't wait to see him in the delivery room. Derek talked a big, tough-guy game, but she'd come to learn he was a softie underneath. The cocky exterior was just an absurdly attractive, but intentionally protective package.

She draped her arms across his shoulders, admiring the glimmer of moonlight on her diamond wedding ring.

"You look beautiful tonight," he said, running his palms over the slick satin of her dress. "Have I told you that?"

"A time or two."

He smiled, a flicker of concern in his deep, loving eyes. "Do you ever regret not having a big wedding like that?"

"Never," she said, recalling their perfect ceremony, nearly nine months back.

In a field of wildflowers on Derek's parents' property, surrounded by friends, family and a whole lot of horses, they'd pledged their love and their lives. And she wouldn't change a single detail. "I think our wedding was better. Blaze and Maisy are probably jealous of us, actually, but we probably shouldn't mention it."

His smile grew. "You think they'll be as happy as we are nine months from now?"

"Impossible," she said. How could anyone be? She sighed a little in sadness for everyone else in the world. "But they did throw one heck of a party."

His smile brushed against her cheek as he dropped kisses along her jaw. "Are you ready for the party we're having here tomorrow?"

A bubble of fresh excitement broke in Allison's chest, and the thrill of victory ran up her spine. Tomorrow was her college graduation party.

She'd gone back to school last fall, and she'd officially completed the rest of the courses needed to earn her degree last week. The degree had come with a promotion to director at the day care where she worked. A perfectly timed graduation as her boss's boss had chosen to retire.

"Do you know how proud I am of you?" he asked.

"So proud?" she asked in the singsong voice she used when telling Bonnie she was so big.

"Yes," he said emphatically, the way he said everything about Allison. "I'm only sorry you won't be around here so much," he said.

The promotion came with longer hours and more weekends. Since she'd be working at Bonnie's day care, they would both be away from Derek for extended periods each day.

Allison was sad about that, too.

"I've been thinking," she said, slipping her fingers into the soft hair at the back of his head. "About a way to use my degree while being around here more. A lot more." Her lips twisted into a mischievous grin. She knew how much Derek would love her idea, even before she said it aloud. She'd been waiting for this night to tell him. All the preliminary details were planned and ready for his input. Because she was good, but together, they were fantastic.

He stilled in response, an eager but curious expression spreading over his handsome face. "Tell me more."

"I could open a preschool here," she said. "We could build it with the money from the sale of Grandma's house. It wouldn't have to be elaborate, and I could handle all the setup inside. I love the day care, and snuggling all those babies, but I also think it would be fun to teach preschool. Just preschool. And with my degree, I can."

Derek kissed her nose, cheeks and forehead. "I love this. I can come home and have lunch with y'all. The kids can learn about our animals. We can buy a pony."

She laughed. "You were going to buy a pony for Bonnie, anyway."

He grinned. "Every little girl needs a pony."

"I thought I would call the school Little Windmills. Because we're on a farm. You have a windmill. Windmills are always spinning, a lot like my future students."

"*We* have a windmill," he corrected, the way he always did when she said anything was his alone. "Let's do this. Tell me how I can help."

"Well, for starters, you can take me to bed and inspire me," Allison teased, then kissed her husband deep and slow. "I have a lot to think about."

She didn't have to ask him twice.

* * * * *

Look for the next book in Julie Anne Lindsey's Heartland Heroes miniseries when Stay Hidden *goes on sale next month.*

And don't miss the previous books in the series:

SVU Surveillance
Protecting His Witness

Available now wherever Harlequin Intrigue books are sold!

WE HOPE YOU ENJOYED
THIS BOOK FROM

⟨H⟩ HARLEQUIN
INTRIGUE

Seek thrills. Solve crimes. Justice served.

Dive into action-packed stories that will keep you
on the edge of your seat. Solve the crime
and deliver justice at all costs.

6 NEW BOOKS AVAILABLE EVERY MONTH!

YOU CAN FIND MORE INFORMATION ON UPCOMING HARLEQUIN TITLES, FREE EXCERPTS AND MORE AT HARLEQUIN.COM.

HICNM1021

"So, tell me who you *think* is stalking you," he said in more of a statement than a question.

She shrugged her shoulders. "I don't know. That's a tough one. There's a guy in one of my classes who creeps me out. I'll be taking notes furiously in class only to get a weird feeling like I'm being watched and then look up to see him staring at me intensely."

"Has he come around the bar?"

"A time or two," she admitted.

"Is he alone?"

"As far as I can tell. He never has worked up the courage to come talk to me, so he takes a table by the dance floor and nurses a beer," she said.

"Any idea what his name is?"

"Derk Waters, I think. I overheard someone say that in a group project when his team was next to mine. By the way, there should be no group projects in college. I end up doing all the work and have to hear complaints from everyone in the process," she said as an aside.

Garrett chuckled. "Maybe you should learn to let others pull their own weight."

She blew out a sharp breath. "And risk a failing grade? No, thanks. Besides, I tried that once and ended up staying up all night to redo someone's work because they slapped their part together."

"Sounds like something you'd do," Garrett said.

"What's that supposed to mean?" She heard the defensiveness in her own voice, but it was too late to reel it in.

"You always were the take-charge type. I'm not surprised you'd pull out a win in a terrible situation."

Well, she really had overreacted. She exhaled, trying to release some of the tension she'd been holding in her shoulders. "Thanks for the compliment, Garrett. It means a lot coming from you. I mean, your opinion matters to me."

"No problem." He shrugged off her comment, but she could see that it meant something to him, too. He picked up his coffee cup and took another sip. "Okay, so we have one creep on the list. What about others?"

"I wouldn't classify this guy as a creep necessarily, but he has followed me out to the parking lot at school more than once. He's a TA, so basically a grad student working for one of my professors. He made it known that he'd be willing to help if I fell behind in class," she said.

Again, that jaw muscle clenched.

"Doesn't he take a hint?"

"Honestly, he's harmless. The only reason I brought him up was because we were talking about school and for some reason he popped into my mind. He's working his way through school and I doubt he'd risk his future if he got caught," she surmised. "Plus, this person is trying to run me off the road."

"You rejected him. That could anger a certain personality type," he said. "What's his name?"

"Blaine something. I don't remember his last name." Up to this point, she hadn't really believed the slimeball could be someone she knew. A cold shiver raced down her spine at the thought. "I've been working under the assumption one of the guys at the bar meant to get a little too friendly."

"We have to start somewhere. I believe my brothers would say the most likely culprit is someone you know. I've heard them say a woman's biggest physical threat is from those closest to her. Boyfriend. Spouse. Someone in her circle." He shot a look of apology. "It's an awful truth."

She issued a sharp sigh. "I can't even imagine who would want to hurt me."

Don't miss
Texas Stalker *by Barb Han,*
available November 2021 wherever
Harlequin Intrigue books and ebooks are sold.

Harlequin.com

HIEXP1021